Self-Help

Self-Help

Stories by
Lorrie Moore

Alfred A. Knopf
New York   1985

THIS IS A BORZOI BOOK
PUBLISHED BY ALFRED A. KNOPF, INC.

Some of the stories were previously published in
Fiction International, MSS Magazine, and *Story Quarterly.*

Library of Congress Cataloging in Publication Data

Moore, Lorrie.
Self-help : stories.

Contents: How to be an other woman—What is seized—
The kid's guide to divorce—[etc.]   I. Title.
PS3563.O6225S4   1985   813'.54   84-48498
ISBN 0-394-53921-4

Manufactured in the United States of America
FIRST EDITION

The purpose of this book is to direct attention to the various ways in which non-backboned animals reproduce . . . Some animals reverse sex, some shoot stimulant darts at each other, and some lose an arm while mating.

—Haig H. Najarian
Sex Lives of Animals Without Backbones

If you start to shake hands with someone who has lost an arm, shake his other hand. If he has lost both arms, shake the tip of his artificial hand (be quick and unembarrassed about it).

—*The Amy Vanderbilt Complete Book of Etiquette*

Give some bones to the dogs and bury the rest around fruit trees . . .

—Phyllis Hobson
Butchering Livestock at Home

Contents

How to Be an Other Woman   1

What Is Seized   23

The Kid's Guide to Divorce   47

How   53

Go Like This   65

How to Talk to Your Mother (Notes)   83

Amahl and the Night Visitors:
A Guide to the Tenor of Love   97

How to Become a Writer   117

To Fill   127

How to Be
an Other Woman

Meet in expensive beige raincoats, on a pea-soupy night. Like a detective movie. First, stand in front of Florsheim's Fifty-seventh Street window, press your face close to the glass, watch the fake velvet Hummels inside revolving around the wing tips; some white shoes, like your father wears, are propped up with garlands on a small mound of chemical snow. All the stores have closed. You can see your breath on the glass. Draw a peace sign. You are waiting for a bus.

He emerges from nowhere, looks like Robert Culp, the fog rolling, then parting, then sort of closing up again behind him. He asks you for a light and you jump a bit, startled, but you give him your "Lucky's Lounge—Where Leisure Is a Suit" matches. He has a nice chuckle, nice fingernails. He lights the cigarette, cupping his hands around the end, and drags deeply, like a starving man. He smiles as he exhales, returns you the matches, looks at your face, says: "Thanks."

He then stands not far from you, waiting. Perhaps for the same bus. The two of you glance furtively at each other, shifting feet. Pretend to contemplate the chemical snow. You are two spies glancing quickly at watches, necks disappearing in the hunch of your shoulders, collars upturned and slowly razoring the cab and store-lit fog like sharkfins. You begin to circle, gauging each other in primordial sniffs, eyeing, sidling, keen as Basil Rathbone.

A bus arrives. It is crowded, everyone looking laughlessly into one another's underarms. A blonde woman in barrettes steps off, holding her shoes in one hand.

You climb on together, grab adjacent chrome posts, and when the bus hisses and rumbles forward, you take out a book.

A minute goes by and he asks what you're reading. It is *Madame Bovary* in a Doris Day biography jacket. Try to explain about binding warpage. He smiles, interested.

Return to your book. Emma is opening her window, thinking of Rouen.

"What weather," you hear him sigh, faintly British or uppercrust Delaware.

Glance up. Say: "It is fit for neither beast nor vegetable."

It sounds dumb. It makes no sense.

But it is how you meet.

At the movies he is tender, caressing your hand beneath the seat.

At concerts he is sweet and attentive, buying cocktails, locating the ladies' lounge when you can't find it.

At museums he is wise and loving, leading you slowly through the Etruscan cinerary urns with affectionate gestures and an art history minor from Columbia. He is kind; he laughs at your jokes.

After four movies, three concerts, and two-and-a-half museums, you sleep with him. It seems the right number of cultural events. On the stereo you play your favorite harp and oboe music. He tells you his wife's name. It is Patricia. She is an intellectual property lawyer. He tells you he likes you a lot. You lie on your stomach, naked and still too warm. When he says, "How do you feel about that?" don't say "Ridiculous" or "Get the hell out of my apartment." Prop your head up with one hand and say: "It depends. What is intellectual property law?"

He grins. "Oh, you know. Where leisure is a suit."

Give him a tight, wiry little smile.

"I just don't want you to feel uncomfortable about this," he says.

Say: "Hey. I am a very cool person. I am tough." Show him your bicep.

When you were six you thought *mistress* meant to put your shoes on the wrong feet. Now you are older and know it can mean many things, but essentially it means to put your shoes on the wrong feet.

You walk differently. In store windows you don't recognize yourself; you are another woman, some crazy interior display lady in glasses stumbling frantic and preoccupied through the mannequins. In public restrooms you sit dangerously flat against the toilet seat, a strange flesh sundae of despair and exhilaration, murmuring into your bluing thighs: "Hello, I'm Charlene. I'm a mistress."

It is like having a book out from the library.

It is like constantly having a book out from the library.

You meet frequently for dinner, after work, split whole liters of the house red, then wamble the two blocks east, twenty blocks south to your apartment and lie sprawled on the living room floor with your expensive beige raincoats still on.

He is a systems analyst—you have already exhausted this joke—but what he really wants to be, he reveals to you, is an actor.

"Well, how did you become a systems analyst?" you ask, funny you.

"The same way anyone becomes anything," he muses. "I took courses and sent out resumes." Pause. "Patricia helped me work up a great resume. Too great."

"Oh." Wonder about mistress courses, certification, resumes. Perhaps you are not really qualified.

"But I'm not good at systems work," he says, staring through and beyond, way beyond, the cracked ceiling. "Figuring out the cost-effectiveness of two hundred people shuffling five hundred pages back and forth across a new four-and-a-half-by-three-foot desk. I'm not an organized person, like Patricia, for instance. She's just incredibly organized. She makes lists for everything. It's pretty impressive."

Say flatly, dully: "What?"

"That she makes lists."

"That she makes lists? You like that?"

"Well, yes. You know, what she's going to do, what she has to buy, names of clients she has to see, et cetera."

"Lists?" you murmur hopelessly, listlessly, your expensive beige raincoat still on. There is a long, tired silence. Lists? You stand up, brush off your coat, ask him what he would like to drink, then stump off to the kitchen without waiting for the answer.

At one-thirty, he gets up noiselessly except for the soft rustle of his dressing. He leaves before you have even quite fallen asleep, but before he does, he bends over you in his expensive beige raincoat and kisses the ends of your hair. Ah, he kisses your hair.

CLIENTS TO SEE
Birthday snapshots
Scotch tape
Letters to TD and Mom

Technically, you are still a secretary for Karma-Kola, but you wear your Phi Beta Kappa key around your neck on a cheap gold chain, hoping someone will spot you for a promotion. Unfortunately, you have lost the respect of all but one of your co-workers and many of your superiors as well, who are working in order to send their daughters to universities so they won't have to be secretaries, and who, therefore, hold you in contempt for having a degree and being a failure anyway. It is like having a degree in failure. Hilda, however, likes you. You are young and remind her of her sister, the professional skater.

"But I hate to skate," you say.

And Hilda smiles, nodding. "Yup, that's exactly what my sister says sometimes and in that same way."

"What way?"

"Oh, I don't know," says Hilda. "Your bangs parted on the side or something."

Ask Hilda if she will go to lunch with you. Over Reuben sandwiches ask her if she's ever had an affair with a married man. As she attempts, mid-bite, to complete the choreography of her chomp, Russian dressing spurts out onto her hands.

"Once," she says. "That was the last lover I had. That was over two years ago."

Say: "Oh my god," as if it were horrible and tragic, then try to mitigate that rudeness by clearing your throat and saying, "Well, actually, I guess that's not so bad."

"No," she sighs good-naturedly. "His wife had Hodgkin's disease, or so everyone thought. When they came up with the correct diagnosis, something that wasn't nearly so awful, he went back to her. Does that make sense to you?"

"I suppose," say doubtfully.

"Yeah, maybe you're right." Hilda is still cleaning Reuben off the backs of her hands with a napkin. "At any rate, who are you involved with?"

"Someone who has a wife that makes lists. She has List-maker's disease."

"What are you going to do?"

"I don't know."

"Yeah," says Hilda. "That's typical."

CLIENTS TO SEE
Tomatoes, canned
Health food toothpaste
Health food deodorant

Vit. C on sale, Rexall
Check re: other shoemaker, 32nd St.

———

"Patricia's really had quite an interesting life," he says, smoking a cigarette.

"Oh, really?" you say, stabbing one out in the ashtray.

Make a list of all the lovers you've ever had.

Warren Lasher
Ed "Rubberhead" Catapano
Charles Deats or Keats
Alfonse

Tuck it in your pocket. Leave it lying around, conspicuously. Somehow you lose it. Make "mislaid" jokes to yourself. Make another list.

Whisper, "Don't go yet," as he glides out of your bed before sunrise and you lie there on your back cooling, naked between the sheets and smelling of musky, oniony sweat. Feel gray, like an abandoned locker room towel. Watch him as he again pulls on his pants, his sweater, his socks and shoes. Reach out and hold his thigh as he leans over and kisses you quickly, telling you not to get up, that he'll lock the door when he leaves. In the smoky darkness, you see him smile weakly, guiltily, and attempt a false, jaunty wave from the doorway. Turn on your side, toward the wall, so you don't have to watch the door close. You hear it thud nonetheless, the jangle of keys and snap of the bolt lock, the footsteps loud, then fading down the staircase, the clunk of the street door, then nothing, all his sounds blending with the city, his face passing namelessly uptown in a bus or a badly heated cab, the room, the whole building you live in, shuddering at the windows as a truck roars by toward the Queensboro Bridge.

Wonder who you are.

"Hi, this is Attila," he says in a false deep voice when you pick up your office phone.

Giggle. Like an idiot. Say: "Oh. Hi, Hun."

Hilda turns to look at you with a what's-with-you look on her face. Shrug your shoulders.

"Can you meet me for lunch?"

Say: "Meet? I'm sorry, I don't eat meat."

"Cute, you're cute," he says, not laughing, and at lunch he gives you his tomatoes.

Drink two huge glasses of wine and smile at all his office and mother-in-law stories. It makes his eyes sparkle and crinkle at the corners, his face pleased and shining. When the waitress clears the plates away, there is a silence where the two of you look down then back up again.

"You get more beautiful every day," he says to you, as you hold your wine glass over your nose, burgundy rushing down your throat. Put your glass down. Redden. Smile. Fiddle with your Phi Beta Kappa key.

When you get up to leave, take deep breaths. In front of the restaurant, where you will stride off in different directions, don't give him a kiss in the noontime throng. Patricia's office is nearby and she likes to go to the bank right around now; his back will stiffen and his eyes dart around like a crazy person's. Instead, do a quick shuffle-ball-chain like you saw Barbra Streisand do in a movie once. Wave gigantically and say: "Till we eat again."

In your office building the elevator is slow and packed and you forget to get off at the tenth floor and have to ride all the way back down again from the nineteenth. Five minutes after you arrive dizzily back at your desk, the phone rings.

"Meet me tomorrow at seven," he says, "in front of Florsheim's and I'll carry you off to my castle. Patricia is going to a copyright convention."

Wait freezing in front of Florsheim's until seven-twenty. He finally dashes up, gasping apologies (he just now got back from the airport), his coat flying open, and he takes you in tow quickly uptown toward the art museums. He lives near art museums. Ask him what a copyright convention is.

"Where leisure is a suit *and* a suite," he drawls, long and smiling, quickening his pace and yours. He kisses your temple, brushes hair off your face.

You arrive at his building in twenty minutes.

"So, this is it?" The castle doorman's fly is undone. Smile politely. In the elevator, say: "The unexamined fly is not worth zipping."

The elevator has a peculiar rattle, for all eight floors, like someone obsessively clearing her throat.

When he finally gets the apartment door unlocked, he shows you into an L-shaped living room bursting with plants and gold-framed posters announcing exhibitions you are too late for by six years. The kitchen is off to one side—tiny, digital, spare, with a small army of chrome utensils hanging belligerent and clean as blades on the wall. Walk nervously around like a dog sniffing out the place. Peek into the bedroom: in the center, like a giant bloom, is a queen-sized bed with a Pennsylvania Dutch spread. A small photo of a woman in ski garb is propped on a nightstand. It frightens you.

Back in the living room, he mixes drinks with Scotch in them. "So, this is it," you say again with a forced grin and an odd heaving in your rib cage. Light up one of his cigarettes.

"Can I take your coat?"

Be strange and awkward. Say: "I like beige. I think it is practical."

"What's wrong with you?" he says, handing you your drink.

Try to decide what you should do:

1. rip open the front of your coat, sending the buttons torpedoing across the room in a series of pops into the asparagus fern;
2. go into the bathroom and gargle with hot tap water;
3. go downstairs and wave down a cab for home.

He puts his mouth on your neck. Put your arms timidly around him. Whisper into his ear: "There's a woman, uh, another woman in your room."

When he is fast asleep upon you, in the middle of the night, send your left arm out slowly toward the nightstand like a mechanical limb programmed for a secret intelligence mission, and bring the ski garb picture back close to your face in the dark and try to study the features over his shoulder. She seems to have a pretty smile, short hair, no eyebrows, tough flaring nostrils, body indecipherably ensconced in nylon and down and wool.

Slip carefully out, like a shoe horn, from beneath his sleeping body—he grunts groggily—and go to the closet. Open it with a minimum of squeaking and stare at her clothes. A few suits. Looks like beige blouses and a lot of brown things. Turn on the closet light. Look at the shoes. They are all lined up in neat, married pairs on the closet floor. Black pumps, blue sneakers, brown moccasins, brown T-straps. They have been to an expensive college, say, in Massachusetts. Gaze into her shoes. Her feet are much larger than yours. They are like small cruise missiles.

Inside the caves of those shoes, eyes form and open their lids, stare up at you, regard you, wink at you from the insoles. They are half-friendly, conspiratorial, amused at this reconnaissance of yours, like little smiling men from the open hatches of a fleet of military submarines. Turn off the light and shut the door quickly, before they start talking or dancing or something. Scurry back to the bed and hide your face in his armpit.

In the morning he makes you breakfast. Something with eggs and mushrooms and hot sauce.

Use his toothbrush. The red one. Gaze into the mirror at a face that looks too puffy to be yours. Imagine using her toothbrush by mistake. Imagine a wife and a mistress sharing the same toothbrush forever and ever, never knowing. Look into the medicine cabinet:

Midol
dental floss
Tylenol
Merthiolate
package of eight emory boards
razors and cartridges
two squeezed in the middle toothpaste tubes: Crest *and* Sensodyne
Band-Aids
hand lotion
rubbing alcohol
three small bars of Cashmere Bouquet stolen from a hotel

On the street, all over, you think you see her, the boring hotel-soap stealer. Every woman is her. You smell Cashmere Bouquet all over the place. That's her. Someone waiting near you for the downtown express: yup, that's her. A woman waiting behind you in a deli near Marine Midland who has smooth, hand-lotioned hands and looks like she skis: good god, what if that is her. Break out in cold sweats. Stare into every pair of flared nostrils with clinical curiosity and unbridled terror. Scrutinize feet. Glance sidelong at pumps. Then look quickly away, like a woman, some other woman, who is losing her mind.

Alone on lunch hours or after work, continue to look every female over the age of twelve straight in the nose and straight in the shoes. Feel your face aquiver and twice bolt out of Bergdorf's irrationally when you are sure it is her at the skirt sale rack choosing brown again, a Tylenol bottle peeking out from the corner of her purse. Sit on a granite wall in the GM plaza and catch your breath. Listen to an old man singing "Frosty the Snowman." Lose track of time.

"You're late," Hilda turns and whispers at you. "Carlyle's been back here twice already asking where you were and if the market survey report has been typed up yet."

Mutter: "Shit." You are only on the T's: Tennessee Karma-Kola consumption per square dollar-mile of investment market. Figures for July 1980–October 1981.

Texas—Fiscal Year 1980
Texas—Fiscal Year 1981
Utah.

It is like typing a telephone directory. Get tears in your eyes.

CLIENTS TO SEE

1. Fallen in love(?) Out of control. Who is this? Who am I? And who is this wife with the skis and the nostrils and the Tylenol and does she have orgasms?

2. Reclaim yourself. Pieces have fluttered away.

3. Everything you do is a masochistic act. Why?

4. Don't you like yourself? Don't you deserve better than all of this?

5. Need: something to lift you from your boots out into the sky, something to make you like little things again, to whirl around the curves of your ears and muss up your hair and call you every single day.

6. A drug.

7. A man.

8. A religion.

9. A good job. Revise and send out resumes.

10. Remember what Mrs. Kloosterman told the class in second grade: Just be glad you have legs.

———

"What are you going to do for Christmas?" he says, lying supine on your couch.

"Oh. I don't know. See my parents in New Jersey, I guess." Pause. "Wanna come? Meet my folks?"

A kind, fatherly, indulgent smile. "Charlene," he purrs, sitting up to pat your hand, your silly ridiculous little hand.

He gives you a pair of leather slippers. They were what you wanted.

You give him a book about cars.

"Ma, open the red one first. The other package goes with it."

"A coffee grinder, why thank you, dear." She kisses you wetly on the cheek, a Christmas mist in her eyes. She thinks you're wonderful. She's truly your greatest fan. She is aging and menopausal. She stubbornly thinks you're an assistant department head at Karma-Kola. She wants so badly, so earnestly, to be you.

"And this bag is some exotic Colombian bean, and this is a chocolate-flavored decaf."

Your father fidgets in the corner, looking at his watch, worrying that your mom should be checking the crown roast.

"Decaf bean," he says. "That's for me?"

Say: "Yeah, Dad. That's for you."

"Who is he?" says your mom, later, in the kitchen after you've washed the dishes.

"He's a systems analyst."

"What do they do?"

"Oh . . . they get married a lot. They're usually always married."

"Charlene, are you having an affair with a married man?"

"Ma, do you have to put it that way?"

"You are asking for big trouble," she says, slowly, and resumes polishing silver with a vehement energy.

Wonder why she always polishes the silver *after* meals.

Lean against the refrigerator and play with the magnets.

Say, softly, carefully: "I know, Mother, it's not something you would do."

She looks up at you, her mouth trembling, pieces of her brown-gray hair dangling in her salty eyes, pink silverware cream caking onto her hands, onto her wedding ring. She stops, puts a spoon down, looks away and then hopelessly back at you, like a very young girl, and, shaking her head, bursts into tears.

"I missed you," he practically shouts, ebullient and adolescent, pacing about the living room with a sort of bounce, like a child who is up way past his bedtime and wants to ask a question. "What did you do at home?" He rubs your neck.

"Oh, the usual holiday stuff with my parents. On New Year's Eve I went to a disco in Morristown with my cousin Denise, but I dressed wrong. I wore the turtleneck and plaid skirt my mother gave me, because I wanted her to feel good, and my slip kept showing."

He grins and kisses your cheek, thinking this sweet.

Continue: "There were three guys, all in purple shirts and paper hats, who kept coming over and asking me to dance. I don't think they were together or brothers or anything. But I danced, and on 'New York City Girl,' that song about how jaded and competent urban women are, I went crazy dancing and my slip dropped to the floor. I tried to pick it up, but finally just had to step out of it and jam it in my purse. At the stroke of midnight, I cried."

"I'll bet you suffered terribly," he says, clasping you around the small of your back.

Say: "Yes, I did."

———

"I'm thinking of telling Patricia about us."

Be skeptical. Ask: "What will you say?"

He proceeds confidently: "I'll go, 'Dear, there's something I have to tell you.'"

"And she'll look over at you from her briefcase full of memoranda and say: 'Hmmmmmmm?'"

"And I'll say, 'Dear, I think I'm falling in love with another woman, and I *know* I'm having sex with her.'"

"And she'll say, 'Oh my god, what did you say?'"

"And I'll say: 'Sex.'"

"And she'll start weeping inconsolably and *then* what will you do?"

There is a silence, still as the moon. He shifts his legs, seems confused. "I'll . . . tell her I was just kidding." He squeezes your hand.

Shave your legs in the bathroom sink. Philosophize: you are a mistress, part of a great hysterical you mean historical tradition. Wives are like cockroaches. Also part of a great historical tradition. They will survive you after a nuclear attack—they are tough and hardy and travel in packs—but right now they're not having any fun. And when you look in the bathroom mirror, you spot them scurrying, up out of reach behind you.

An hour of gimlets after work, a quick browse through Barnes and Noble, and he looks at his watch, gives you a peck, and says: "Good night. I'll call you soon."

Walk out with him. Stand there, shivering, but do not pout. Say: "Call you 'later' would sound better than 'soon.' 'Soon' always means just the opposite."

He smiles feebly. "I'll phone you in a few days."

And when he is off, hurrying up Third Avenue, look down at your feet, kick at a dirty cigarette butt, and in your best juvenile mumble, say: "Fuck you, jack."

Some nights he says he'll try to make it over, but there's no guarantee. Those nights, just in case, spend two hours showering, dressing, applying makeup unrecognizably, like someone in drag, and then, as it is late, and you have to work the next day, climb onto your bed like that, wearing perfume and an embarrassing, long, flowing, lacy bathrobe that is really not a bathrobe at all, but a "hostess loungecoat." With the glassed candle by your bed lit and burning away, doze off and on, arranged with excruciating care on top of the covers, the window lamp on in the living room, the door unlocked for him in case he arrives in a passionate flurry, forgetting his key. Six blocks from Fourteenth Street: you are risking your life for him, spread out like a ridiculous cake on the bed, waiting with the door unlocked, thinking you hear him on the stairs, but no. You should have a corsage, you think to yourself. You should have a goddamned orchid pinned to the chest of your long flowing hostess coat, then you would be appropriately absurd. Think: What has happened to me? Why am I lying like this on top of my covers with too much Jontue and mascara and jewelry, pretending casually that this is how I always go to bed, while a pervert with six new steak knives is about to sneak through my unlocked door. Remember: at Blakely Falls High, Willis Holmes would have done anything to be with you. You don't have to put up with this: you were second runner-up at the Junior Prom.

A truck roars by.

Some deaf and dumb kids, probably let out from a dance at the school nearby, are gathered downstairs below your window, hooting and howling, making unearthly sounds. You guess they are laughing and having fun, but they can't hear themselves, and at night the noises are scary, animal-like.

Your clock-radio reads 1:45.

Wonder if you are getting old, desperate. Believe that you have really turned into another woman:

your maiden aunt Phyllis;

some vaporish cocktail waitress;

a glittery transvestite who has wandered, lost, up from the Village.

When seven consecutive days go by that you do not hear from him, send witty little postcards to all your friends from college. On the eighth day, when finally he calls you at the office, murmuring lascivious things in German, remain laconic. Say: *"Ja . . . nein . . . ja."*

At lunch regard your cream of cauliflower soup with a pinched mouth and ask what on earth he and his wife *do* together. Sound irritated. He shrugs and says, "Dust, eat, bicker about the shower curtain. Why do you ask?"

Say: "Gee, I don't know. What an outrageous question, huh?"

He gives you a look of sympathy that could bring a dead cat back to life. "You're upset because I didn't call you." He reaches across the table to touch your fingers. Pull your hand away. Say: "Don't flatter yourself." Look slightly off to one side. Put your hand over your eyes like you have a headache. Say: "God, I'm sorry."

"It's okay," he says.

And you think: Something is backward here. Reversed. Wrong. Like the something that is wrong in "What is wrong with this picture?" in kids' magazines in dentists' offices. Toothaches. Stomachaches. God, the soup. Excuse yourself and hurry toward the women's room. Slam the stall door shut. Lean back against it. Stare into the throat of the toilet.

Hilda is worried about you and wants to fix you up with a cousin of hers from Brooklyn.

Ask wearily: "What's his name?"

She looks at you, frowning. "Mark. He's a banker. And what the hell kind of attitude is that?"

———

Mark orders you a beer in a Greek coffee shop near the movie theater.

"So, you're a secretary."

Squirm and quip: "More like a sedentary," and look at him in surprise and horror when he guffaws and snorts way too loudly.

Say: "Actually, what I really should have been is a dancer. Everybody has always said that."

Mark smiles. He likes the idea of you being a dancer.

Look at him coldly. Say: "No, nobody has ever said that. I just made it up."

All through the movie you forget to read the subtitles, thinking instead about whether you should sleep with Mark the banker. Glance at him out of the corner of your eye. In the dark, his profile seems important and mysterious. Sort of. He catches you looking at him and turns and winks at you. Good god. He seems to be investing something in all of this. Bankers. Sigh. Stare straight ahead. Decide you just don't have the energy, the interest.

"I saw somebody else."

"Oh?"

"A banker. We went to a Godard movie."

"Well . . . good."

"Good?"

"I mean for you, Charlene. You should be doing things like that once in a while."

"Yeah. He's real rich."

"Did you have fun?"

"No."

"Did you sleep with him?"

"No."

He kisses you, almost gratefully, on the ear. Fidget. Twitch. Lie. Say: "I mean, yes."

He nods. Looks away. Says nothing.

———

Cut up an old calendar into week-long strips. Place them around your kitchen floor, a sort of bar graph on the linoleum, representing the number of weeks you have been a mistress: thirteen. Put X's through all the national holidays.

Go out for a walk in the cold. Three little girls hanging out on the stoop are laughing and calling to strange men on the street. "Hi! Hi, Mister!" Step around them. Think: They have never had orgasms.

A blonde woman in barrettes passes you in stockinged feet, holding her shoes.

There are things you have to tell him.

CLIENTS TO SEE
1.   This affair is demeaning.
2.   Violates decency. Am I just some scampish tart, some tartish scamp?
3.   No emotional support here.
4.   Why do you never say "I love you" or "Stay in my arms forever my little tadpole" or "Your eyes set me on fire my sweet nubkin"?

The next time he phones, he says: "I was having a dream about you and suddenly I woke up with a jerk and felt very uneasy."

Say: "Yeah, I hate to wake up with jerks."

He laughs, smooth, beautiful, and tenor, making you feel warm inside of your bones. And it hits you; maybe it all boils down to this: people will do anything, anything, for a really nice laugh.

Don't lose your resolve. Fumble for your list. Sputter things out as convincingly as possible.

Say: "I suffer indignities at your hands. And agonies of duh feet. I don't know why I joke. I hurt."

"That is why."

"What?"

"That is why."

"But you don't really care." Wince. It sounds pitiful.

"But I do."

For some reason this leaves you dumbfounded.

He continues: "You know my situation . . . or maybe you don't." Pause. "What can I do, Charlene? Stand on my goddamned head?"

Whisper: "Please. Stand on your goddamned head."

"It is ten o'clock," he says. "I'm coming over. We need to talk."

What he has to tell you is that Patricia is not his wife. He is separated from his wife; her name is Carrie. You think of a joke you heard once: What do you call a woman who marries a man with no arms and no legs? Carrie. Patricia is the woman he lives with.

"You mean, I'm just another one of the fucking gang?"

He looks at you, puzzled. "Charlene, what I've always admired about you, right from when I first met you, is your strength, your independence."

Say: "That line is old as boots."

Tell him not to smoke in your apartment. Tell him to get out.

At first he protests. But slowly, slowly, he leaves, pulling up the collar on his expensive beige raincoat, like an old and haggard Robert Culp.

Slam the door like Bette Davis.

Love drains from you, takes with it much of your blood sugar and water weight. You are like a house slowly losing its electricity, the fans slowing, the lights dimming and flickering; the clocks stop and go and stop.

———————

At Karma-Kola the days are peg-legged and aimless, collapsing into one another with the comic tedium of old clowns, nowhere fast.

In April you get a raise. Celebrate by taking Hilda to lunch at the Plaza.

Write for applications to graduate schools.

Send Mark the banker a birthday card.

Take long walks at night in the cold. The blonde in barrettes scuttles timelessly by you, still carrying her shoes. She has cut her hair.

He calls you occasionally at the office to ask how you are. You doodle numbers and curlicues on the corners of the Rolodex cards. Fiddle with your Phi Beta Kappa key. Stare out the window. You always, always, say: "Fine."

What Is Seized

My mother married a cold man. Not that he couldn't make her laugh, because he could do that: he'd pull some antic in the living room—sing nursery rhymes in an Italian accent, safety-pin an olive to his lapel, tell jokes about chickens, elephants, or morons. And because he performed with the local musical theater group every spring and fall, and usually got the funny parts, he sometimes practiced in the kitchen while she was doing stuff, making her grin in spite of herself, making her giggle into the batter bowl. My father taught clarinet and math at the high school in town. He seemed to know how to get people to like him, to do crazy stunts with furniture or time-rate problems. I would usually hear about these secondhand. People in Crasden seemed to think he was amazing somehow. Special, they said. Talented. But when he made love to my mother, he kept his eyes closed the whole time, turned his head away from her, and afterward would give her a hard, angry gaze, roll stiffly over to his side of the bed, face the wall, shake her off of him with a shudder or a flinch if she kissed his shoulder, rubbed his arm, lay a palm against his bare back. She told me this before she died. She just stared off to one side at the drapes and told me.

We lived on a lake and used to hear the water bang and slurp at the dock pilings at night. We also had a rowboat tied and afloat at the end, which would clunk against the wood when the water got rough. "Old man boat, old man boat," James would sometimes sing to be funny, instead of "Old Man River," which my mother had taught us. James and I shared the large bed in the lakeside room upstairs, in the morning often waking up staring into each other's eyes, and at night spending hours

listening for the underwater world in the lake to come magically
to life, when no one was looking, when it was pitch black and
still except for the quietest rocking, and the good, shy fish would
put on pink and orange jackets and smile and go to balls, with
violins and oriental fans.

James was my foster brother—half Indian, half Pennsylvania Catholic. His parents had met in college. In 1958 his
father returned for good to a small city north of Calcutta, and
his mother had a nervous breakdown, came to Crasden to live,
but later got sick and died. James became a public ward and
came to live with us when he was five and I was four; we never
talked about his past. He had smooth black hair and a wide
white smile. I thought it was funny that his lips were brown
and that every night he scraped his tongue with a wooden
scraper. "Be kind to James," my mother said. "He is your brother
now." Sometimes he would cry, but not that often.

The rooms in our house were like songs. Each had its own
rhythmic spacing and clutter, which if you crossed your eyes
became a sort of musical notation, a score—clusters of eighth
notes, piles of triplets, and the wooden roundness of doorways,
like clefs, all blending in a kind of concerto. Or sometimes, as
with the bathroom, with its motif of daisies and red plastic, they
created a sort of jingle, something small, likable, functional. It
was the bookcase in the living room that seemed particularly
symphonic, the books all friendly with one another, a huge
chorus of them in a hum; they stood packed behind glass doors
with loose metal knobs. My mother also kept photo albums,
scrapbooks, yearbooks on the bottom shelf of the case, along
with the big, heavy books like *Smith's World History* and the
Golden Treasury of Children's Stories. In one book she had
black and white pictures of herself, starting from when she was
little. Gray, empty days I would take that book out and look
at it. By the time I was nine, I knew all the pictures by heart.
To stare at them, to know those glimpses, I felt, was to know

her, to become her, to make my mother a woman with adventures, a woman in a story, a book, a movie. The photos somehow seemed powerful. Sometimes I still look at them, with a cup of coffee, with the television on.

A photo where she is six and has bangs bleached pale from the sun. She is in a white sundress, standing next to a large tricycle, squinting and frowning into the camera. Crabface. That's what my mother called it: "Oh yeah, there's me, ole crabface, pouting for soda pop."

My mother liked to sing, but she would wait until my father wasn't around because he would correct her pitch and straighten her posture and insist she use her lungs and diaphragm better. "Don't sing like a disembodied mule. You should use your whole rib cage. And sitting on the piano bench, she would poker-stare straight ahead at the sheet music and play the C above middle C over and over again with one finger, a sort of hypnosis. "Go mow the lawn, Enrico," she would say sometimes. Which was a joke, because my father's real name was Sam and because we really had no lawn, just a craggy, pine-needled slope, which galloped wildly from the road down to the lake. On the other side of the house was a slow, tiny stream, which trickled and glided gingerly over rocks, like something afraid of hurting itself.

At night with the lights out, after she had heard our prayers, my mother would sing to James and me, and we thought she was great. She'd sing "Down by the Old Mill Stream" or some Cole Porter hit she knew from college. She loved Frank Sinatra. She would stand by our bed, crooning imitations into one of the bedposts as if it were a microphone, and afterward we would clap in the dark until our hands stung. (At the end of "Pennies from Heaven," she would place a penny on each post for us to find in the morning.) "Thank you, thank you," she would whisper with a low, wonderful laugh, smiling and bending over us

to wetly kiss our cheeks, her hair down, long, black, and sweep-
ing against my chest and chin, smelling soapy and dry. And if
the moon was out it lit up the lake, and the lake light shone
into the room through the slats of the blinds, tentatively striping
her hair and face or the arm of her sweater. And as she moved—
to kiss James, to tuck in the blankets—the stripes moved up and
down her. When she left she always kept the door slightly un-
latched, the lamp from the hall framing the door in cracks of
light interrupted only by hinges. She always called in a whisper,
"Good night my sweet sparrows," that expression only later in
my life seeming silly or indulgent or mad. And often James
would be on his back next to me humming late into the night,
invisible in the dark, singing the words to "Old Devil Moon"
when he could remember them, or sometimes just whispering,
"Hey, Lynnie, how does it go again?" his legs jiggling under the
sheets.

A photo where she is eight and her hair is darker, wavier,
and she already has the bones of her adult face beginning to
grow inside, cheekbones awakening behind the skin. She is grinning in a striped shirt with her arm around Uncle Don, her
blank-faced little brother, in front of a house they lived in just
outside of Syracuse, a white house with a closed-in front porch
and a brick chimney painted white, two large tamaracks on either
side, their branches dangling curved and protective over the
roof, like large mustaches. Uncle Don comes up to her chin.

My father played Liza Doolittle's father in *My Fair Lady*
and the knight with the dog in *Camelot*. On Sunday afternoons
my mother would bring us to watch them rehearse in the Crasden High School auditorium, but in 1956, so that it was new
and strong and maroon and velvet and hadn't lost its polish.
I loved the dark slope of it, and would gallop along the rows of
empty flip-bottom seats as if they were my own private corridors.
The director would pace out in front of the stage, a few feet

beyond the orchestra pit. At early rehearsals they just used a pianist, a puffy woman named Mrs. Beales who took many trips to the ladies' room. "The entire action to the right and further downstage, downstage," the director was always shouting, waving both arms like a semaphore. He had thick, white, horse-mane hair that he combed straight back from his brow but that nevertheless flopped into his eyes from time to time. He wore white shoes and usually dressed in something of pale blue silk. My father would say things during scene cuts on stage that we couldn't hear but that made everyone laugh—a talky, theatrical, group laugh, filled with ho-ho's and oh-no's and affectionate hissing and stomping. Sometimes the director would wear sunglasses and prop them on top of his head and say, "Oh shit, let's take a break." And then the lights would go up and the actors would head for the cafeteria two long marble hallways away, and as the school was empty and lit up like a bowling alley, you could hear the echo of their steps and their loud chatter, the woman who played Liza Doolittle still screeching "Aow," adding, "Did you phone the babysitter, Ron?" and Professor Higgins, not with them but seated on the stage's edge, eating a sandwich he had brought, his legs dangling, sneakers thumping against each other, like a Little Leaguer. During these breaks, James and I would dash up onto the stage to see my father, and, if it was a dress rehearsal, we would giggle at his orange face or his wig or his fake eyebrows arched way up into his forehead. But then we would be struck by shyness when he would say, "Hi, kids," but look past us, over our heads, then turn and head busily backstage to take care of something. Standing there on the stage, we would turn and look out onto the hill of auditorium seats, spot my mother in the tenth row where we had left her reading a book, and she would wave and we would wave, then we'd race to her, like racing home, and climb hungrily all over her lap, as if looking for something. Sometimes we played with the bobby pins in her hair, which she used to hold it in a twist in the back, making antennae, making antlers, my mother allowing it all. "Your father is a talented man," my mother said, sounding like my teachers at school who said similar things to me, my mother sensing our disappointment in never getting his attention for very long. "Talented men have very busy heads. They may seem unkind sometimes." And I would think about this for a long time afterward, chewing my nails, writing letters.

A photo in which she is nine and dressed for a ballet class in a long-sleeved black leotard, in the living room in front of the fireplace. She is doing an arabesque, one arm bent slightly over her head, one arm out to the side; because it is a front view, only one leg shows, and she looks something like an amputee, the tip of her ballet shoe just visible above the outline of her shoulder, her whole body leaning into the camera as her eyes gaze off to one side of it, looking half sorrowful, half comical. "She looks like a greasehead," James said once, sitting next to me, taking note of the tight wet way her hair was pulled off her face into a bun. "You're a greasehead," I said, nurturing fantasies of becoming a ballerina myself, and I punched him in the leg. He moved farther back on the couch, a little away from me, and just chewed his gum harder. Sometimes when we had fights, I would say I'm sorry, and sometimes he would. He liked to look at the pictures, too.

"Cold men destroy women," my mother wrote me years later. "They woo them with something personable that they bring out for show, something annexed to their souls like a fake greenhouse, lead you in, and you think you see life and vitality and sun and greenness, and then when you love them, they lead you out into their real soul, a drafty, cavernous, empty ballroom, inexorably arched and vaulted and mocking you with its echoes —you hear all you have sacrificed, all you have given, landing with a loud clunk. They lock the greenhouse and you are as tiny as a figure in an architect's drawing, a faceless splotch, a blur of stick limbs abandoned in some voluminous desert of stone."

"Dear Mom," I wrote back. *"I am coming home on the 23rd, so should be there for the candlelight service on Sunday. Hope all is going well. Exams are merciless. See you soon."*

A photo of my mother when she is fourteen and the adult bones are at last there—stark cemented lines, startling as the curves in a mountain road, from eye to jaw, her skin lineless, and although she is not smiling there is no sadness in her face, simply an inquiring, a wide stare of scrutiny, a look of waiting, of preparedness.

My mother was the only mother I knew who wore her hair long. Sometimes she would wear it in a single braid that hung like a dark tail, marbled with auburn sun streaks, down the middle of her back; other times she wore it in two side braids that would swing back and forth when she bent over. "You look like a featherhead Indian lady," James would tell her. He was just being made aware of the distinction between India Indian and the kind you saw on TV. "How," my mother would joke, holding up a hand. And James, not getting it, would tug impatiently at her braids and say, "Because of these, because of these."

She is fifteen and has Tonied her hair into a wild frizz that dances, dark and frenetic, way out beyond the barrettes she uses to clamp it down. She is sitting on a bench in a park somewhere, eating an ice cream cone, blue jeans rolled up mid-calf, legs spread wide and feet pigeon-toed, ankles caved outward, and she is hunched a bit forward with her cone, making a crazy face that involves sticking out her tongue and crossing her eyes.

There were nights my parents fought, woke us up with their fighting, and James would put his pillow over his face and I would lie wide-eyed, terrified and paralyzed by my father's bellowing, the doors slamming, something metal always clinking somewhere to the floor, the pounding on the walls, and my mother's "Oh god, oh god, just leave, why don't you."

One afternoon, the day after one of these night fights, I brought my friend Rachel home on the bus with me. We walked in the kitchen door and I reminded her to wipe her feet. Down the hallway that led to the bathroom I suddenly saw my mother, sitting on the toilet with the door wide open, her legs and hips bare and white, her underwear coiled at her ankles, her long hair all unbraided, a mane of unbrushed ripples floating out and downward toward her waist. She didn't move when we walked in. She just sat there in an old black shirt like some obscene statue, her head leaning frozenly on her hands, her elbows propped on her knees.

"Is that your *mother?*" whispered Rachel.

And I said maybe it was and maybe it wasn't.

My mother never saw us, but continued to stare like a drunkard at something on the floor just ahead of her.

"Come on," I said, and led Rachel upstairs to my room where James, on the bed, was reading a bird encyclopedia: cowbirds, starlings, cuckoos. "Look at this," he said. "A blue-booted boobie." And we looked and saw it was just some dumb black-faced bird. And then all three of us played "Careers" and Rachel bought a farm and lots of happiness, but I was the first man on the moon and loaded up on stars, winning everything.

Her high school graduation picture. The yearbook caption reads, "Salutatorian" and "Best All-Around." Her friends write things like, "Beautiful Anna, we will miss you off in Chicago, come back to visit." "The Windy City has a treat coming its way. Good luck." "Stay as sweet as you are. Remember the Bluebird Dance. We had fun. Good luck at U. of Chi. Love, Barbara."

That night, or was it another night, my mother came into our room late after we had already tucked ourselves in and she laid our schoolbooks on the floor next to our bed and then stood in the doorway awhile, looking wraithlike, silent, in a long white sleeveless nightgown, one bare arm dangling loosely at her side, the other bent upward, hand cupped around the back of her neck, thoughtfully, her head tilted toward the dangling arm, her dark unpinned hair obscuring one shoulder like the hood of a cape. And there was a bird outside on the lake, hooting, calling, and it was the only sound, and James murmured groggily, "That's a loon, a ruby-throated loon," and my mother turned and disappeared until morning.

"Your father wrote music, too, you know, but he never shared it with us," my mother said, a bit breathlessly, as I smoothed out her blankets. "Music ultimately left him unstirred. Like a god irritated with his own tinkerings. Despite his talent, or perhaps because of it, he heard only the machinery, the clanking and spitting. He felt nothing. No compassion." She coughed. "You would think creating something would necessarily be an act of love or compassion."

"Mother," I said, remembering the nurse's instructions. "Perhaps you should take your pill now."

She leaves behind all her friends, including Barbara. A picture of this, with streamers and cake and wine bottles. At college she falls in love with a sophomore named Jacob Fish and works toward a degree in fine arts. After four years she leaves him, inexplicably goes back home, paints and designs sets for a local Syracuse theater group. *Kismet. South Pacific.* See the scenery. She also sings in the chorus; that's her, there.

I remember overhearing a brief snatch of a fight my parents had once. Or rather my mother was crying and having difficulty explaining why to my father, as he seemed angry and distant, she said, and soon he was screaming at her that she should stop her goddamn crying and perhaps get some exercise

for a change. At this my mother cried even harder and my father
stormed out of the house. But the next day, and several times a
week for years afterward, my mother was running along the
lake in sweatclothes and old sneakers she didn't mind getting
wet. Once in a while I went with her, jogging next to her, watching her breasts float up and down beneath her sweatshirt, imi-
tating the way she breathed in and out with quick snorts. Twice
we saw dead birds washed up on shore and we stopped to look
at their bedraggled carcasses, their eyes already crawling with
small black bugs. "What is beautiful is seized," my mother said.
"My grandmother used to tell me that."

   Scotch-taped to my mother's scrapbook is a thumb-sized
lavender picture viewer, which, when you look through the
eyehole and hold it up to a light, magnifies a tiny picture of
her and Jacob Fish on New Year's Eve at a big hotel in the
Catskills. On the outside of the viewer is printed in gold script,
"Kiamesha Lake, N.Y.," and there is a small gold chain attached
to it, so you can hang it somewhere or twirl it around your fingers. Inside of it, when you peer through, my mother is standing
next to Jacob Fish, both done up like prom royalty, my mother
in a strapless apricot dancing gown, her hair piled up on top of
her head, fastened with pins and one pale rose, and Jacob Fish,
short and tow-headed, just about her height, with a navy blue bow
tie, a kindness and graciousness in his face, which, I can tell, made
my mother happy, made her smile, timelessly holding his arm
in the little lavender capsule.

   Saturdays were motherless—she went in to Crasden to shop
—and my father would sometimes make pancakes and play cards
with us: "Go Fish" and "War." Sometimes he would do tricks:
we would pick a card and he wouldn't know what it was and
then we would put it back in the deck, which he would shuffle,
cut, make piles, rows, and columns with, and eventually he
would find our card. All his card tricks were variations of this.

Sometimes it seemed that we were the ones to find it ourselves, as when we held the deck and he'd karate-chop it, the sole remaining card in our hand being, miraculously, the one we had chosen. "Aw, how'dya do that?" James would want to know and he would grab the cards and try to figure it out as my father put on an exaggerated, enigmatic smile, shrugged his shoulders, folded his arms. "I'll never tell, will I, Lynnie?" My dad would wink at me.

I never wanted to know. It was enough to sit in the living room in my pajamas and smell pancakes and be reassured that my father was special. To discover or expose the wheels and pulleys behind the tricks, I knew, would be to blacken Saturdays and undo my father. If his talents, his magic, his legerdemain, didn't remain inimitable, unknowable, if they weren't protected and preserved, what could he possibly be, to us, for us, what could he do?

A picture of Mom and Jacob Fish on a beach. Mom's one-piece is black like her hair and the water is gray and the sand is white. There are buckets, a small shovel, and a blanket. Jacob Fish holds a fistful of sand over Mom's head. She laughs with her eyes closed, a momentary shutting out, the only way sometimes one can laugh.

The fall I turned ten, my father played Billy Bigelow in the Crasden Playhouse production of *Carousel*. Halfway through the show Billy Bigelow sings a song about his plans for his child to be, warbling through a lilting list of parental love promises. My mother brought us to the Sunday afternoon rehearsals (the real performance was too late for us, she said) and sat stiff and pinched through that song, staring narrowly at my father as he walked through it, following the snow-haired director's commands for the placement of his feet ("Damn it, Sam . . . you sing like a god, but you just can't dance"). Off to one side two stagehands were painting a merry-go-round red and green.

"Bad colors," my mother said, shaking her head critically. A blonde woman a few seats away piped up: "Last week somebody stole all the good paint. Our budget is tight."

"What is beautiful is seized," murmured my mother, and the blonde woman looked at her oddly and said, "Yeah, I guess," and after a few minutes got up and left. Years later my mother would say to me: "That song your father sang in *Carousel.* What wonderful lies. He never spent time with you kids, never sang to you or took you places."

And when she said it, it became true. But only then, when she said it. Until then it seemed Dad was just Dad, was somehow only what he was supposed to be.

A picture of Jacob Fish standing by a river with a suitcase in one hand and a hat in another. That was the City River, opposite the train station, my mother said. The suitcase was hers. So was the hat. He was trying to look dignified and worldly and had requested props.

She cries, slumped over at her dressing table, and dreams that someone comes up behind her and bends down to hold her, to groan and weep into her neck with her, to turn her around and lift up her face, kiss her eyes, mouth on water, on cheek, on hair. But there is no one, just my father, sitting way across the room from her, in a white and rose upholstered chair (something later moved to my room at college, something I would sit in, stare at), an icy anger tucked behind his face, locked up like a store after hours, a face laced tight as a shoe. His arms are crossed behind his head like a man on vacation, but he is not relaxed. His features arrange themselves in straight, sharp lines.

"Your numbness," my mother cries softly, "is something perhaps you cannot help. It is what the world has done to you. But your coldness. That is what you do to the world."

He picks up a porcelain pill box on the lamp table, hurls

and shatters it against the wall. "That's what I have to say to you," he says. "I won't do your little dances." And he walks out, slamming the door.

I only heard parts of this. She told me the rest years later when she was dying, and I spent hours brushing and brushing her hair. She liked me to do that, always managing a smile and sinking back into her pillow. "My legs, Lynnie. Can you do my legs today, dear?" she would ask. And I'd take the Norelco razor from the nightstand drawer, pull up the covers from the foot of the bed, and glide the razor up and down her calves. She liked her legs smooth and hairless, and I think she liked the metallic friction and buzz of it. That, too, made her smile.

A picture of my parents on bikes before they were married. They are at a gas station where they have stopped to fill up their tires with air. Mom smiles. Dad makes a goofy face, both hands on the handlebars. Both of them wear long, Jamaica-style shorts. An Esso sign behind them is missing the *O*. Yiddish for "eat," my mother told me once.

"They want to take things and destroy them," my mother sighed the same month she died, when we were talking of our lake house, which had been sold at first to a funeral home and then bought by the federal government, who tore it down for vaguely military purposes no one ever bothered to explain.
"They want my hair," she said another day, winking weakly at me when a nurse came in with scissors and suggested a haircut. My mother shook her head, but the nurse's air was insistent.
"I *don't* think she wants one," I said, and the nurse looked at me dumbly and padded out on the soundless rubber soles those who surround the dying always wear.

My mother coming into our room at night. My childhood sometimes simply a series of images of her swirling into the doorway, in white, over and over again, coming to hear our prayers, to sing us songs, to whisper that she loved us, to kiss me wetly on the mouth, hair dangling, making a tent in which just our faces, hers and mine, lived and breathed forever. She'd rub my nose, and James's too, and whisper, "See you tomorrow," and at the doorway, "Good night, my sparrows."

She dreams that he is trying to kill her. That he has a rifle and is calling her out of the bathroom. In the bathroom she has knives and axes. She bolts awake and he is looking at her, chilly, indifferent. "Your face," she says. "My god. It is a murderer's face."

"What the hell are you talking about?" he says.

The year after *Carousel* was *The Music Man,* and the woman who played Marian the librarian used to call our house fairly regularly, purring like older women do at babies. She would ask if my *Daddy* was home.

"My father's not here," I almost always said, even if I knew he was upstairs with lesson plans. I think of all the things I did as a child, this was the boldest.

She would ask me to tell him that Marcia called. Sometimes I would. I'd knock on the door to his study, walk in, and say: "Marcia called. She wanted you to know."

And he would turn and look at me vacantly, as if he wasn't quite sure who I was talking about, and then say, "Oh, right. About rehearsal. Thanks." And he would turn his back to me and continue working at his desk, and I would just stand there in the doorway, staring at the back of his sweater. It seemed when he corrected papers and things that he always wore the same Norwegian sweater: green with a chain of rectangularized gold reindeer around the top, across his back and shoulders.

"Did you want anything else?" He would twist around again in his seat and lower his glasses.

And I would say, "No. I mean yes."

"What?"

"I forgot," I would say, and turn and flee.

In the wedding photos they wear white against the murky dark of trees. They are thin and elegant. They have placid smiles. The mouth of the father of the bride remains in a short, straight line. I don't know who took these pictures. I suppose they are lies of sorts, revealing by omission, by indirection, by clues such as shoes and clouds. But they tell a truth, the only way lies can. The way only lies can.

Another morning, I heard my parents up early in the bathroom, my dad shaving, getting ready to leave for school.

"Look," he sighed in a loud whisper. "I really can't say that I'll never leave you and the kids or that I'll never make love to another woman—"

"Why not?" asked my mother. "Why can't you say that?" Even her anger was gentle, ingenuous.

"Because I don't feel that way."

"But . . . can't you just say it anyway?"

At this I like to imagine that my parents met each other's gaze in the medicine cabinet mirror, suddenly grinning. But later in the hospital bed, holding my hand and touching each of my nails slowly with her index finger, my mother said to me, "Your father. He was in a dance. And he just couldn't dance." Earlier that year she had written me: "That is what is wrong with cold people. Not that they have ice in their souls—we all have a bit of that—but that they insist their every word and deed mirror that ice. They never learn the beauty or value of gesture. The emotional necessity. For them, it is all honesty before kindness, truth before art. Love is art, not truth. It's like painting scenery."

These are the things one takes from mothers. Once they die, of course, you get the strand of pearls, the blue quilt, some of the original wedding gifts—a tray shellacked with the invitation, an old rusted toaster—but the touches and the words and the moaning the night she dies, these are what you seize, save, carry around in little invisible envelopes, opening them up quickly, like a carnival huckster, giving the world a peek. They will not stay quiet. No matter how you try. No matter how you lick them. The envelopes will not stay glued.

"Dear Mom, The extra courseload makes life hectic, but I think I'm getting used to it. Spring break is the 19th. Yikes. So much to do before I can leave. See you then."

When I was thirteen, my mother left rice burning on the stove and half-tried to drown herself in the lake. At seven o'clock, my father not home yet and James late at Chess Club, I stepped out the back door and called for her. It was March and the lake was not even completely melted yet—a steely slate green with a far-off whitish center, like some monstrous wound. I walked down to the dock; sometimes she went down there "for air" just before making dinner. I found her on the shore—we really had no beach, just a stoney straggle along the waterline for jogging and rock-skipping. She was on her back, her blouse soaked and transparent, her black hair plastered in strings across her face, water lapping at her like an indifferent cat. She was clutching fistfuls of gravel and smearing them across her cheeks, down the front of her body, her legs still but her mouth opening and closing noiselessly, twisted and stretched, the first of two such expressions of hers I would witness. I couldn't move. Even years later I would see that face—in my own, in photos, in mirrors, that severely sculpted anguish moving behind mine, against mine, against my less dramatic bones and thick, squarish mouth, struggling to emerge. I cried. I didn't know what to do. I ran back to the house, burst into the kitchen, and saw my father, who had just gotten home, scraping black smoking rice angrily from the bottom of the pan. "Mom, it's Mom," I panted, and pointed toward the lake. And he shouted, "What?" and hurried out and down the path.

At eight o'clock an ambulance came and took her away. She came back, however, the next morning, looking a little pale and raccoon-eyed, trudging upstairs on my father's arm. She glanced at me, it seemed, apologetically.

My father spent that next day down on the dock, singing out at the lake, something Italian, a Puccini aria or something. He actually did this about twice a year while I was growing up, a way of releasing things inside of him, my mother said, in a way, he hoped, that would not disturb the neighbors (who were a quarter of a mile away on each side). Sometimes I would stare out the back-door window and be able to make out the outline of him, sometimes sitting, but more often pacing the dock cross-planks, his voice floating up toward the house. But not his school voice or his theater voice—this was something else, a throbbing, pained vibrato, like some creature that lived inside of him that he didn't understand, that embarrassed him, that he didn't know quite what to do with. Sometimes I would leave the house and go for a walk in the opposite direction, up past the road, through the woods, across the old train tracks. There was a boarded-up building, a small factory of some sort, and an unusable old road, bordered with ancient gaslight posts with the jets yanked from them, hollowed as skeleton eyes, and James and I both would sometimes go up there to look for berries and make up stories and dares. Dare to run to the door and back. Dare to tear off the PRIVATE PROPERTY poster. Dare to climb in the window. To touch the electric fence. To this day it remains a mystery to me what was inside the place, or what its original function was. All nailed and shuttered and papered with NO TRESPASSING signs. Sometimes we swore we heard noises inside—James would call it grumbling, but I always thought of it as being like my father on the dock, blockaded and alone, singing in its strange foreign language, a need to be exploded somehow, a need to disgorge an aria over the lake. Finally some people came from the city and did blow it up. Laced it up with dynamite and blasted out

its corners, its flat roof, its broken windowpanes, its black insides
laid bare and smoldering in the daylight, neighbors well beyond
a quarter-mile off hearing it at breakfast, kids talking about it
at school, and bits of nails and plaster we found later stuck like
shrapnel in the posts of the gaslights, like a war, like there had
been a war.

Another photo of my mother in her wedding dress, standing next to her mother, whose smile and hat are too big for her
face; she seems vaguely eyeless, noseless. And her daughter looks
not at the camera but off to one side somewhere.

I was fifteen when my father left us and my mother had
her mastectomy. Both things happened suddenly, quietly, without announcement. As if some strange wind rushed in and swept
things up into it, then quickly rushed out again; it simply left
what it left.

When your parents divide, you, too, bifurcate. You cleave
and bubble and break in two, live two lives, half of you crying
every morning on the dock at sunrise, black hair fading to dusky
gray, part of you traveling off to some other town where you
teach school and tell jokes in an Italian accent in a bar and make
people laugh.

And when your mother starts to lose her mind, so do you.
You begin to be afraid of people on the street. You see shapes—
old men and spiders—in the wallpaper again like when you were
little and sick. The moon's reflection on the lake starts to look
to you like a dead fish floating golden belly up. Ask anyone. Ask
anyone whose mother is losing her mind.

When I was sixteen, I came home from school and found
my mother drunk in her bathrobe, lying flat on the coffee table
in the living room, spread out on top of the magazines. She was
out of control with laughter, hysterical wine-tears trickling out
of the swollen slits of her eyes.

"Mom, come upstairs. Let me put you to bed," I said, setting down my books and helping her upstairs. She was leaning on me, still laughing helplessly. "My god," she said. "They lopped off my breasts, can you believe it? Lopped them right—" and she made a quick motion with her hand in the air.

I tucked her in and kissed her face and she cried into the neck of my blouse. "I'm cold. I'm thirsty. Don't leave me, honey. You're warm. If you leave I'll have to put on a sweater."

"Get some sleep," I said softly, pulling up the blue quilt, drawing the blinds, standing in the doorway, just a moment, to watch her fall asleep, the lake beating like a giant watery heart against the dock.

She takes long, silent showers, slumped against the ceramic wall, the steady jets of water bouncing off one of her shoulders, splashing against the plastic curtain, shampoo lather drizzling down into her mouth.

"Even his I love you's," she said, "were like tiny daggers, like little needles or safety pins. Beware of a man who says he loves you but who is incapable of a passionate confession, of melting into a sob."

I tuck her in. I kiss her.

A series of pictures here of mothers and daughters switching places—women switching places to take care of one another. You, the daughter, becoming the mother, the Ceres, and she the daughter, kidnapped to hell, and you roam the earth to find her, to mourn her, leaving the trees and grain to wither, having no peace, you have no peace.

"What is beautiful is seized," my mother said a final time, speaking of my father, whom she said had been destroyed by too many women, a heart picked over, scratched at, taken, lost. "It came to me in bulky bandages, seeming much larger, much more than it really was."

———

My mother, thin and gray in a nightgown, staring off and away, not at the camera.

"You reach a point," she wrote me once, "where you cannot cry anymore, and you look around you at people you know, at people your own age, and they're not crying either. Something has been taken. And they are emptier. And they are grateful."

When my mother died, her groaning woke the elderly woman in the bed next to hers who was supposed to have her pancreas operated on the next day. "What is happening?" cried the old woman, sleepless and distraught. Something had seized my mother in the back, arched it, stiffened her limbs, her mouth a gash across her face, revealing only her teeth, yellowed fine as old piano keys. An awful astonishment pervaded her features, her bones, as if she never really believed death would be like this, a bludgeoning by tubes and contractions, and by the time— only a minute—the nurses responded to my shouts and came running, the sweat and urine soaking into the sheets already seemed cool and old and my mother's eyes were wide as eggs and she was dead. I clutched at things—her robe, a plastic pitcher, a cup—and looking around, around the room, the window, wondered where she had gone, she must still be, had to be near, somewhere, and the lady with the pancreas, beyond the screen next to the bed, had heard it all and now wept loudly, inconsolably, and they gave her a sleeping pill although she pushed it away, saying, "Oh, please, god, no." Nothing moved. I bent over the bed. "Mom," I whispered, kissing her lips, surgical carts rackety in the hallway, a voice in the ceiling paging Dr. Davis Dr. Davis to the nurses' station, figures in white slowly gathering around me, hands on my shoulders, hard, false as angels. "Mom," I breathed.

Jacob Fish came to the funeral with a pretty brunette

woman who looked like a high school French teacher. He seemed somehow like a nice man. At the end of the burial, he escorted the woman back to the car and then went off by himself, over to a tree, and ran his hands through his hair. I never really got a chance to talk with him, although I'm not certain what we would have talked about. When he was through at the tree and had thrust his hands back into his pockets, he rejoined the woman in the car and drove off.

My father did not bring anyone with him. He came up to me and hugged me tightly and for a moment the red rushed to both of our eyes. "Lynnie," he said, and I stepped to one side. I looked away from him. I looked at his shoes. I looked at the clouds. "I loved her more than you think," he said, and I listened for the needles, the safety pins. James, home from medical school and standing next to me, shook my dad's hand, then quickly embraced him. Everyone was dressed in black. "So much black, so much black," I kept repeating like some nervous mynah bird.

That night James and I left all the casseroles at my mother's apartment and went out and got drunk at a Howard Johnson's. James made me smile reminding me of the time when I was little and insisted that if you were in the woods and had to go to the bathroom really badly, all you had to do was eat a piece of bread; it would absorb everything, and you wouldn't have to go anymore.

"James," I asked him, carefully. "Do you ever think about your other mother?"

"No," he said quickly, like a doctor.

I looked at him, dismayed, confused.

"I don't know," he sighed and signaled the waiter. "I guess it's not basic to me. God, I can't get my feet all tied up in that. Why should I?"

"I'm not sure." I looked at my lap, at my shoes. I reached under the table for my purse. "Check's on me," I said.

"Dear Mom. Thanks for the cookies. I got them yesterday. Was sorry to hear about the hospital thing. Hope you're feeling better. I've got tests by the millions! Love, Lynnie."

Driving back from dropping James off at the airport, I catch a glimpse of my face in the mirror. It seems old, with too much makeup. I feel stuck, out of school, working odd jobs, like someone brooding, hat in hand in an anteroom, waiting for the future as if it were some hoop-skirted belle that must gather up its petticoats, float forward, and present itself to me. I wonder what else I could have written, those winters, looking out and seeing snow lining the elm grove like an arthritis and finding no words. I didn't lie: there were a lot of tests; I had a lot of tests.

The roads are empty and I am driving fast. I think of my father, imagine him long ago at night casually parting my mother's legs with the mechanical indifference of someone opening a cupboard. And I say to myself: I will leave every cold man, every man for whom music is some private physics and love some unsteppable dance. I will try to make them regret. To make them sad. I am driving back toward my tiny kitchen table and I will write this: forgiveness lives alone and far off down the road, but bitterness and art are close, gossipy neighbors, sharing the same clothesline, hanging out their things, getting their laundry confused.

"That's how much it costs, Miss," says the attendant at the gas station where I stop, looking rather numbly at the price on the pump.

"Oh," I say and fumble for my wallet. The oil cans stacked against an old truck tire are wordless, hard, collusive. But the triangular plastic flags strung at one end of the island flutter and ripple in the wind, flapping to get my attention, my compassion, like things that seem to want to sing but can't, things that almost tear themselves in trying to fly, like rainbow-colored birds, hung by string and their own feet.

The Kid's Guide
to Divorce

Put extra salt on the popcorn because your mom'll say that she needs it because the part where Inger Berman almost dies and the camera does tricks to elongate her torso sure gets her every time.

Think: Geeze, here she goes again with the Kleenexes.

She will say thanks honey when you come slowly, slowly around the corner in your slippers and robe, into the living room with Grandma's old used-to-be-salad-bowl piled high. I made it myself, remind her, and accidentally drop a few pieces on the floor. Mittens will bat them around with his paws.

Mmmmm, good to replenish those salts, she'll munch and smile soggily.

Tell her the school nurse said after a puberty movie once that salt is bad for people's hearts.

Phooey, she'll say. It just makes it thump, that's all. Thump, thump, thump—oh look! She will talk with her mouth full of popcorn. Cary Grant is getting her out of there. Did you unplug the popper?

Pretend you don't hear her. Watch Inger Berman look elongated; wonder what it means.

You'd better check, she'll say.

Groan. Make a little *tsk* noise with your tongue on the roof of your mouth. Run as fast as you can because the next commercial's going to be the end. Unplug the popper. Bring Mittens back in with you because he is mewing by the refrigerator. He'll leave hair on your bathrobe. Dump him in your mom's lap.

Hey baby, she'll coo at the cat, scratching his ears. Cuddle close to your mom and she'll reach around and scratch one of your ears too, kissing your cheek. Then she'll suddenly lean forward, reaching toward the bowl on the coffee table, carefully so as not to disturb the cat. I always think he's going to realize faster than he does, your mom will say between munches, hand to hand to mouth. Men can be so dense and frustrating. She will wink at you.

Eye the tube suspiciously. All the bad guys will let Cary Grant take Inger Berman away in the black car. There will be a lot of old-fashioned music. Stand and pull your bathrobe up on the sides. Hang your tongue out and pretend to dance like a retarded person at a ball. Roll your eyes. Waltz across the living room with exaggerated side-to-side motions, banging into furniture. Your mother will pretend not to pay attention to you. She will finally say in a flat voice: How wonderful, gee, you really send me.

When the music is over, she will ask you what you want to watch now. She'll hand you the *TV Guide.* Look at it. Say: The Late, Late Chiller. She'll screw up one of her eyebrows at you, but say *please, please* in a soft voice and put your hands together like a prayer. She will smile back and sigh, okay.

Switch the channel and return to the sofa. Climb under the blue afghan with your mother. Tell her you like this beginning cartoon part best where the mummy comes out of the coffin and roars, *CHILLER!!* Get up on one of the arms of the sofa and do an imitation, your hands like claws, your elbows stiff, your head slumped to one side. Your mother will tell you to sit back down. Snuggle back under the blanket with her.

When she says, Which do you like better, the mummy or the werewolf, tell her the werewolf is scary because he goes out at night and does things that no one suspects because in the day he works in a bank and has no hair.

What about the mummy? she'll ask, petting Mittens.

Shrug your shoulders. Fold in your lips. Say: The mummy's just the mummy.

With the point of your tongue, loosen one of the chewed, pulpy kernels in your molars. Try to swallow it, but get it caught in your throat and begin to gasp and make horrible retching noises. It will scare the cat away.

Good god, be careful, your mother will say, thwacking you on the back. Here, drink this water.

Try groaning root beer, root beer, like a dying cowboy you saw on a commercial once, but drink the water anyway. When you are no longer choking, your face is less red, and you can breathe again, ask for a Coke. Your mom will say: I don't think so; Dr. Atwood said your teeth were atrocious.

Tell her Dr. Atwood is for the birds.

What do you mean by that? she will exclaim.

Look straight ahead. Say: I dunno.

The mummy will be knocking down telephone poles, lifting them up, and hurling them around like Lincoln Logs.

Wow, all wrapped up and no place to go, your mother will say.

Cuddle close to her and let out a long, low, admiring *Neato*.

The police will be in the cemetery looking for a monster. They won't know whether it's the mummy or the werewolf, but someone will have been hanging out there leaving little smoking piles of bones and flesh that even the police dogs get upset and whine at.

Say something like gross-out, and close your eyes.

Are you sure you want to watch this?

Insist that you are not scared.

There's a rock concert on Channel 7, you know.

Think about it. Decide to try Channel 7, just for your mom's sake. Somebody with greasy hair who looks like Uncle Jack will be saying something boring.

Your mother will agree that he does look like Uncle Jack. A little.

A band with black eyeshadow on will begin playing their guitars. Stand and bounce up and down like you saw Julie Steinman do once.

God, why do they always play them down at their crotches? your mom will ask.

Don't answer, simply imitate them, throwing your hair back

and fiddling bizarrely with the crotch of your pajama bottoms. Your mother will slap you and tell you you're being fresh.

Act hurt. Affect a slump. Pick up a magazine and pretend you're reading it. The cat will rejoin you. Look at the pictures of the food.

Your mom will try to pep you up. She'll say: Look! Pat Benatar! Let's dance.

Tell her you think Pat Benatar is stupid and cheap. Say nothing for five whole minutes.

When the B-52's come on, tell her you think *they're* okay.

Smile sheepishly. Then the two of you will get up and dance like wild maniacs around the coffee table until you are sweating, whooping to the oo-ah-oo's, jumping like pogo sticks, acting like space robots. Do razz-ma-tazz hands like your mom at either side of your head. During a commercial, ask for an orange soda.

Water or milk, she will say, slightly out of breath, sitting back down.

Say shit, and when she asks what did you say, sigh: Nothing.

Next is Rod Stewart singing on a roof somewhere. Your mom will say: He's sort of cute.

Tell her Julie Steinman saw him in a store once and said he looked really old.

Hmmmm, your mother will say.

Study Rod Stewart carefully. Wonder if you could make your legs go like that. Plan an imitation for Julie Steinman.

When the popcorn is all gone, yawn. Say: I'm going to bed now.

Your mother will look disappointed, but she'll say, okay, honey. She'll turn the TV off. By the way, she'll ask hesitantly like she always does. How did the last three days go?

Leave out the part about the lady and the part about the beer. Tell her they went all right, that he's got a new silver dart-board and that you went out to dinner and this guy named Hudson told a pretty funny story about peeing in the hamper. Ask for a 7-Up.

How

> *So all things limp to-*
> *gether for the only pos-*
> *sible.*
> *—Beckett*
> Murphy

Begin by meeting him in a class, in a bar, at a rummage sale. Maybe he teaches sixth grade. Manages a hardware store. Foreman at a carton factory. He will be a good dancer. He will have perfectly cut hair. He will laugh at your jokes.

A week, a month, a year. Feel discovered, comforted, needed, loved, and start sometimes, somehow, to feel bored. When sad or confused, walk uptown to the movies. Buy popcorn. These things come and go. A week, a month, a year.

Make attempts at a less restrictive arrangement. Watch them sputter and deflate like balloons. He will ask you to move in. Do so hesitantly, with ambivalence. Clarify: rents are high, nothing long-range, love and all that, hon, but it's footloose. Lay out the rules with much elocution. Stress openness, non-exclusivity. Make room in his closet, but don't rearrange the furniture.

And yet from time to time you will gaze at his face or his hands and want nothing but him. You will feel passing waves of dependency, devotion, and sentimentality. A week, a month, a year, and he has become your family. Let's say your real mother is a witch. Your father a warlock. Your brothers twin hunchbacks of Notre Dame. They all live in a cave together somewhere.

His name means savior. He rolls into your arms like Ozzie and Harriet, the whole Nelson genealogy. He is living rooms and turkey and mantels and Vicks, a nip at the collarbone and you do a slow syrup sink into those arms like a hearth, into those living rooms, well hello Mary Lou.

Say you work in an office but you have bigger plans. He wants to go with you. He wants to be what it is that you want to be. Say you're an aspiring architect. Playwright. Painter. He shows you his sketches. They are awful. What do you think?

Put on some jazz. Take off your clothes. Carefully. It is a craft. He will lie on the floor naked, watching, his arms crossed behind his head. Shirt: brush on snare, steady. Skirt: the desultory talk of piano keys, rocking slow, rambling. Dance together in the dark though it is only afternoon.

Go to a wedding. His relatives. Everyone will compare weight losses and gains. Maiden cousins will be said to have fattened embarrassingly. His mother will be a bookkeeper or a dental hygienist. She will introduce you as his *girl*. Try not to protest. They will have heard a lot about you. Uncles will take him aside and query, What is keeping you, boy? Uncomfortable, everywhere, women in stiff blue taffeta will eye you pitifully, then look quickly away. Everyone will polka. Someone will flash a fifty to dance with the bride and she will hike up her gown and flash back: freshly shaven legs, a wide rolled-out-barrel of a grin. Feel spared. Thought you two'd be doing this by now, you will hear again. Smile. Shrug. Shuffle back for more potato salad.

It hits you more insistently. A restlessness. A virus of discontent. When you pass other men in the street, smile and stare them straight in the eye, straight in the belt buckle.

Somehow—in a restaurant or a store—meet an actor. From Vassar or Yale. He can quote Coriolanus's mother. This will seem good. Sleep with him once and ride home at 5 a.m. crying

in a taxicab. Or: don't sleep with him. Kiss him good night at
Union Square and run for your life.

Back at home, days later, feel cranky and tired. Sit on the
couch and tell him he's stupid. That you bet he doesn't know who
Coriolanus is. That since you moved in you've noticed he rarely
reads. He will give you a hurt, hungry-to-learn look, with his
James Cagney eyes. He will try to kiss you. Turn your head. Feel
suffocated.

When he climbs onto the covers, naked and hot for you,
unleash your irritation in short staccato blasts. Show him your
book. Your aspirin. Your clock on the table reading 12:45. He
will flop back over to his side of the bed, exasperated. Maybe
he'll say something like: Christ, what's wrong? Maybe he won't.
If he spends too long in the bathroom, don't ask questions.

The touchiest point will always be this: he craves a family,
a neat nest of human bowls; he wants to have your children.
On the street he pats their heads. In the supermarket they gather
around him by the produce. They form a tight little cluster of
cheeks and smiles and hopes. They look like grapes. It will all
be for you, baby; reel, sway backward into the frozen foods.
An unwitting sigh will escape from your lips like gas. He will
begin to talk about a movie camera and children's encyclopedias,
picking up size-one shoes in department stores and marveling in
one high, amazed whistle. Avoid shopping together.

He will have a nephew named Bradley Bob. Or perhaps a
niece named Emily who is always dressed in pink and smells of
milk and powder and dirty diapers, although she is already three.
At visits she will prance and squeal. She will grab his left leg
like a tree trunk and not let go. She will call him nunko. He
will know tricks: pulling dimes from her nose, quarters from
her ears. She will shriek with glee, flapping her hands in front

of her. Leg released, he will pick her up, carry her around like a prize. He is the best nunko in town.

Think about leaving. About packing a bag and slithering off, out the door.

But it is hot out there. And dry. And he can look somehow good to you, like Robert Goulet in a bathing suit.

No, it wouldn't be in summer.

Escape into books. When he asks what you're reading, hold it up without comment. The next day look across to the brown chair and you will see him reading it too. A copy from the library that morning. He has seven days. He will look over the top and wink, saying: Beat you.

He will seem to be listening to the classical music station, glancing quickly at you for approval.

At the theater he will chomp Necco wafers loudly and complain about the head in front of him.

He will ask you what *supercilious* means.

He will ask you who Coriolanus is.

He might want to know where Sardinia is located.

What's a *croissant?*

Begin to plot your getaway. Envision possibilities for civility. These are only possibilities.

A week, a month, a year: Tell him you've changed. You no longer like the same music, eat the same food. You dress differently. The two of you are incongruous together. When he tells you that he is changing too, that he loves your records, your teas, your falafel, your shoes, tell him: See, that's the problem. Endeavor to baffle.

Pace around in the kitchen and say that you are unhappy.

But I love you, he will say in his soft, bewildered way, stirring the spaghetti sauce but not you, staring into the pan as if waiting for something, a magic fish, to rise from it and say: That is always enough, why is that not always enough?

You will forget whoever it was that said never trust a thought that doesn't come while walking. But clutch at it. Apartments can shrink inward like drying ponds. You will gasp. Say: I am going for a walk. When he follows you to the door, buzzing at your side like a fly by a bleeding woman, add: *alone.* He will look surprised and hurt and you will hate him. Slam the door, out, down, hurry, it will be colder than you thought, but not far away will be a bar, smoky and dark and sticky with spilled sours. The bartender will be named Rusty or Max and he will know you. A flashy jukebox will blare Jimmy Webb. A balding, purple-shirted man to your left will try to get your attention, mouthing, singing drunkenly. Someone to your right will sniffle to the music. Blink into your drink. Hide behind your hair. Sweet green icing will be flowing down. Flowing, baby, like the Mississippi.

Next: there are medical unpleasantries. Kidneys. He will pee blood. Say you can't believe it. When he shows you later, it will be dark, the color of meat drippings. A huge invisible fist will torpedo through your gut, your face, your pounding heart.

This is no time to leave.

There will be doctor's appointments, various opinions. There is nothing conclusive, just an endless series of tests. He will have jarred urine specimens in the refrigerator among the eggs and peanut butter. Some will be in salad dressing bottles. They will be different colors: some green, some purple, some brown. Ask which is the real salad dressing. He will point it out and smile helplessly. Smile back. He will begin to laugh and so will you. Collapse. Roll. Roar together on the floor until you cannot laugh anymore. Bury your face in the crook of his neck. There will be nothing else in the world you can do. That night lie next to each other, silent, stiff, silvery-white in bed. Lie like sewing needles.

Continue to doctor-hop. Await the reports. Look at your watch. If ever you would leave him. Look at your calendar. It wouldn't be in autumn.

There is never anything conclusive, just an endless series of tests.

Once a week you will feel in love with him again. Massage his lower back when it is aching. Lay your cheek against him, feeling, listening for his kidneys. Stay like that all night, never quite falling asleep, never quite wanting to.

The thought will occur to you that you are waiting for him to die.

You will meet another actor. Or maybe it's the same one. Begin to have an affair. Begin to lie. Have dinner with him and his Modigliani-necked mother. She will smoke cigars, play with the fondue, discuss the fallacy of feminine maternal instinct. Afterward, you will all get high.

There is never anything conclusive, just an endless series of tests.

And could you leave him tripping merrily through the snow?

You will fantasize about a funeral. At that you could cry. It would be a study in post-romantic excess, something vaguely Wagnerian. You would be comforted by his lugubrious sisters and his dental hygienist mom. The four of you in the cemetery would throw yourselves at his grave's edge, heaving and sobbing like old Israeli women. You, in particular, would shout, bare your wrists, shake them at the sky, foam at the mouth. There would be no shame, no dignity. You would fly immediately to Acapulco and lounge drunk and malodorous in the casinos until three.

After dinners with the actor: creep home. Your stomach will get fluttery, your steps smaller as you approach the door. Neighbors will be playing music you recall from your childhood —an opera about a pretty lady who was bad and cut a man's hair in his sleep. You recall, recall your grandfather playing it with a sort of wrath, his visage laminated with Old Testament righteousness, the violins warming, the scenario unfolding now as you stand outside the door. Ray pawned off my ten dresses: it cascades like a waterfall. Dolly-la, Dolly-la: it is the wail, the next to the last good solo of a doomed man.

Tiptoe. It won't matter. He will be sitting up in bed looking empty. Kiss him, cajole him. Make love to him like never before. At four in the morning you will still be awake, staring at the ceiling. You will horrify yourself.

Thoughts of leaving will move in, bivouac throughout the living room; they will have eyes like rodents and peer out at you from under the sofa, in the dark, from under the sink, luminous glass beads positioned in twos. The houseplants will appear to have chosen sides. Some will thrust stems at you like angry limbs. They will seem to caw like crows. Others will simply sag.

When you go out, leave him with a sinkful of dirty dishes. He will slowly dry them with paper towels, his skin scalded red beneath the wet, flattened hair of his forearms. You will be tempted to tell him to leave them, or to use the terrycloth in the drawer. But you won't. You will put on your coat and hurry away.

When you return, the bathroom light will be on. You will see blouses of yours that he has washed by hand. They will hang in perfect half-inches, dripping, scolding from the shower curtain rod. They will be buttoned with his Cagney eyes, faintly hooded, the twinkle sad and dulled.

Slip quietly under the covers; hold his sleeping hand.

There is never anything conclusive.

At work you will be lachrymose and distracted. You will shamble through the hall like a legume with feet. People will notice.

Nightmares have seasons like hurricanes. Be prepared. You will dream that someone with a violin case is trailing you through the city. Little children come at you with grins and grenades. You may bolt awake with a spasm, reach for him, and find he is not there, but lost in his own sleep, somnambulant, is roaming through the apartment like an old man, babbling gibberish, bumping into tables and lamps, a blanket he has torn from the bed wrapped clumsily around him, toga-style. Get up. Go to him. Touch him. At first he will look at you, wide-eyed, and not see. Put your arms around his waist. He will wake and gasp and cry into your hair. In a minute he will know where he is.

Dream about rainbows, about escapes, about wizards. Your past will fly by you, event by event, like Dorothy's tornadoed neighborhood, past the blown-out window. Airborne. One by one. Wave hello, good-bye. Practice.

Begin to call in sick. Make sure it is after he has already left for work. Sit in a rocking chair. Stare around at the apartment. It will be mid-morning and flooded in a hush of sunlight. You rarely see it like this. It will seem strangely deserted, premonitory. There will be apricots shrunk to buttons on the windowsill. A fly will bang stupidly against the panes. The bed will lie open, revealed, like something festering, the wrinkles in the sheets marking time, marking territory like the capillaries of a map. Rock. Hush. Breathe.

On the night you finally tell him, take him out to dinner. Translate the entrees for him. When you are home, lying in bed together, tell him that you are going to leave. He will look panicked, but not surprised. Perhaps he will say, Look, I don't care who else you're seeing or anything: what is your reason?

Do not attempt to bandy words. Tell him you do not love him anymore. It will make him cry, rivulets wending their way into his ears. You will start to feel sick. He will say something like: Well, you lose some, you lose some. You are supposed to laugh. Exhale. Blow your nose. Flick off the light. Have a sense of humor, he will whisper into the black. Have a heart.

Make him breakfast. He will want to know where you will go. Reply: To the actor. Or: To the hunchbacks. He will not eat your breakfast. He will glare at it, stir it around the plate with a fork, and then hurl it against the wall.

When you walk up Third Avenue toward the IRT, do it quickly. You will have a full bag. People will seem to know what you have done, where you are going. They will have his eyes, the same pair, passed along on the street from face to face, like secrets, like glasses at the opera.

This is what you are.
Rushing downstairs into the steamy burn of the subway.
Unable to look a panhandler in the pan.

You will never see him again. Or perhaps you will be sitting in Central Park one April eating your lunch and he will trundle by on roller skates. You will greet him with a wave and a mouth full of sandwich. He will nod, but he will not stop.

There will be an endless series of tests.

A week, a month, a year. The sadness will die like an old dog. You will feel nothing but indifference. The logy whine of a cowboy harmonica, plaintive, weary, it will fade into the hills slow as slow Hank Williams. One of those endings.

Go Like This

*If an elephant missteps and dies
in an open place, the herd will
not leave him there . . .*
—Lewis Thomas
The Lives of a Cell

I have written before. Three children's books: *William, William Takes a Trip, More William.* Perhaps you've heard of them. In the first, William gets a duck, builds it a house with a doorbell. In the second, William goes to Wildwood and has a good time. In the third, William finds a wildebeest in his closet. It messes up his room. Life is tough all around.

I was planning a fourth book, but I didn't know finally what William should do. So instead, I am writing of rational suicide—no oxymoron there. I eschew all contradictions, inconsistencies, all stripes with plaids. I write as a purist, a lover of skim milk, a woman who knows which pieces of furniture look right together in the living room. A month ago I was told I have cancer. It was not the clean, confined sort I might have hoped for, suspended neatly in my breast with its slippery little convolutions turned tortuously inward on itself, hardened, wizened to a small extractable walnut. Or even two. It had spread through my body like a clumsy uninvited guest who is obese and eats too much, still finding, filling rooms. I tried therapy for three weeks, wearing scarves, hiding hairbrushes. I turned up the stereo when rushing into the bathroom to be sick. Blaine heard my retching above the Mozart only twice. Mommyouallright? Her voice had a way of drifting through the door, a small, misplaced melody that had lost its way, ending up in a room full of plumbing and decaying flesh, cavorting innocently with the false lilac aerosol and the mean stench of bile and undigested foods. Okay, honey, I'm okay. Hell, I'm okay.

- - -

Dr. Torbein said that many women go like this for months and improve. Live many years after. Go Christmas shopping, have birthday cakes, all those simple pleasures, now you certainly would like that wouldn't you, Elizabeth?

I am not a skinny child with charge cards, I said. You can't honestly expect me to like this. And please: don't call me Elizabeth.

He was taken aback, vaguely annoyed. Ad lib unpleasantries, my, my. He did not have lines for this. He took off his glasses, no, perhaps you'd call them spectacles, and stared at me over his clipboard, the glare one gives a fractious child who is not going to get ice cream. This is not going to be easy, he informed me. (No maple walnut.) But women have survived much greater damage than you have suffered, much worse odds, worse pain than this.

Well, waddaya know, I cheered heartily. Bully for them.

Now Elizabeth, he scolded. He started to raise a finger, then changed his mind. Go like this, he said instead, demonstrating that I should lift my arm as high as possible over my head so he could examine tissue, feel for further lumps or something. He began to whistle "Clementine."

Ouch! I shrieked. He stopped whistling.

Dreadful sorry, he murmured, trying to probe more gently.

I try not to look at my chest. It is ravaged, paved over, mowed down by the train tracks and parking lots of the Surgical Way. I know there are absences, as if the hollows were the surreptitious marks of a child's spoon in tomorrow night's dessert. The place where I thought my soul was located when I was five is no longer there.

I haven't worn falsies since junior high, I smiled and told the doctor, my future spreading before me, a van Ruisdael cemetery. Thank god I don't have to take gym like y'know wadda mean, doc?

– – –

Joanie, Joanie, my friend with the webbed toes, why do I make Dr. Torbein so uncomfortable, don't you think he'd be used to this by now, he must get it all the time, even if he doesn't get it *all* all the time, you know what I mean? (Joanie smiles and looks at her feet a lot.) I mean, he's got his glasses so far down here, see, that he has to tuck two of his chins back into the recesses of his throat in order to read The Clipboard, which seems to grow out of his gut like some visceral suburbia, and unless we are speaking of the ferrous content of blood, he is utterly ill at ease with irony and gets twitches, like this, see? (Horrid, feeble humor.)

Joanie groans and rolls her eyeballs like Howdy Doody. Jesusmaryandjoseph, Liz, she sighs. (Only Catholics can say that.) You're really getting silly.

Even wit deteriorates, I say, my eye running fast out of twinkles.

— — —

I have decided on Bastille Day. It is a choice of symbol and expedience. Elliott will have time enough before he begins teaching again in the fall. Blaine will not go to camp this year and can spend some time with Elliott's folks upstate. As it will be unbearably hot, I'm sure, I will tell everyone to wear light clothes. No black, no ties, no hats, no coats. The dead are cruel to inflict that misery in July. Open-toed shoes and parasols de rigueur, I will tell everyone. (Ditto: pastels, seersucker, flasks and vials of Scotch, cocaine.) They should require little prompting. They're enlightened. They've seen others go like this before. They read the papers, see the movies, watch the television broadcasts. They know how it's done. They know what for. It's existential. It's Hemingway. It's familiar. They know what to do.

When I told Elliott of my suicide we were in the kitchen bitching at each other about the grease in the oven. Funny, I had

planned on telling him a little differently than No one has
fucking cleaned this shithole in weeks Elliott I have something
to tell you. It wasn't exactly Edna Millay.

I have lain. In bed. So many nights. Thinking of how it
would be when I told him. And plotting, ruminating, remembering the ways our bodies used to love each other, touch, waltz.
Now my body stands in the corner of the gym by the foul lines
and extra crepe paper and doesn't get asked to dance at all.
Blighted, beaten, defeated friend. I rock it, hold it like a sick
child; alone, my body and I, we weep for the missing parts. I
never question Elliott's reluctance to have sex with me. It is not
the same body to him, with his simple, boyish perceptions of
the physical. It's okay, I say, but I look at the curve of his bones,
the freckled skin of his back, something wildly magical still,
something precious. I always think he's the first one to drop off
to sleep at night, but I have often awoken in the morning to
find the hand lotion bottle on the floor by his side of the bed, so
I know it's not always so. It's like some rude poem of my stupidity, of this space grown between us. (Oh, Elliott, I am so
sorry.) I return the lotion to the bathroom sometimes only to
discover it by the bed again the next morning. I never hear
him. (Elliott, is there nothing I can do? Is there nothing?)

He looked a little white, standing there by the oven. He
took my hand, kissed it, held it between his, patted it. Let's think
about it for a day or two or whatever. Then we'll discuss it
further.
    Then we'll discuss it further, I repeated.
    Yes, he said.
    Yes, I said.

But we didn't. Not really. Oh, it drifted piecemeal into
subsequent dialogues like a body tossed out to sea and washed

days later back into shore, a shoe there, a finger here, a breast-bone in weed tide-bumping against the sand. But we never truly discussed it, never truly. Instead, allusions, suggestions, clues, silent but palpable, crawled out of the night ocean, as in a science fiction movie: black and slow they moved in and arranged themselves around the apartment like precocious, breathing houseplants, like scavengers.

I heard Elliott last night. He thought I was asleep, but I could see his motions under the covers and the tense drop of his jaw. I thought of Ivan Ilych who, dying, left his overweight wife in the master bedroom (with the knickknacks?) to sleep alone in a small room next to the study.

Darkness. The late spring sky has strangely emptied. The moon rummages down in the alleyway like somebody's forgotten aunt.

— — —

I have invited our closest friends over tonight, seated them around the living room, and told them that I wanted to die, that I had calculated how much Seconal was required. They are a cool intellectual lot. They do not gasp and murmur among themselves. I say I have chosen suicide as the most rational and humane alternative to my cancer, an act not so much of self-sacrifice as of beauty, of sparing. I wanted their support.

You have obviously thought this out, says Myrna, the poet whom I have loved since childhood for the burlap, asthma-rasp of her voice, making decisions of a lifetime with the speed of deli orders. She can dismiss lovers, choose upholstery, sign on dotted lines, and fly to Olbia faster than anyone I know. She is finality with a hard obsidian edge. We are dealing, she continues, with a mind, as Williams put it, like a bed all made up. You have our love and our support, Liz.

I look around and try to smile gratefully as Myrna seems to speak for everyone, even without conferring. A miracle, that woman. There appears to be no dissent.

I say, Well now, and sip my Scotch and think of my bed in the next room strangled in the twists of sheets and blankets, edges dragging on the floor. I am not afraid of death, I decide to add. I am afraid of what going on like this will do to me and to my daughter and to my husband.

Elliott, arranged next to me on the sofa, looks at his fingers, which tip to tip form a sort of steeple between his knees.

I am getting into the swing of it. I tell them the cancer is poisoning at least three lives and that I refuse to be its accomplice. This is not a deranged act, I explain. Most of them have known for quite a while my belief that intelligent suicide is almost always preferable to the stupid lingering of a graceless death.

There is silence, grand as Versailles. It seems respectful.

Shennan, Algonquin princess with black braids and sad eyes, stands and says in the oratory deadpan of sixth-grade book reports: I think I can speak for Liz when I say that suicide can be, often is, the most definitive statement one can make about one's life, to say that it's yours and that you are not going to let it wither away like something decaying in a refrigerator drawer. As it is Liz's life to do with as she pleases, so it is her death. As long as Liz and I have known one another, I think we have both realized that she would probably be a suicide. It is no inchoate fancy. It is Liz's long-held vision, a way of meeting one's death squarely, maturely. It is an assertion of life, of self.

(Ah, Shennan dear, yes, but didn't I always say that seventy-one would be better than forty-two, in love as I am with prime numbers, those curious virginal devils, and they could always say, ah, yes, she died in her prime—even at seventy-one—good god I'm really getting awful, Joanie, what did I tell you, babe?)

Shennan finishes by saying it is the culmination of a life

philosophy, the triumph of the artist over the mortal, physical world.

It will possibly be the most creative act Liz has ever accomplished, adds my husband. I mean, it could be viewed that way.

He swallows with some difficulty, his wonderful Adam's apple gliding up and down his throat, a tiny flesh elevator. I think of the warm beers, unfinished books, the buttonless sweaters, and the miscarriages upstairs. I wonder if he could be right.

I think it is beautiful she is doing this for me, Elliott adds as a further announcement. He squeezes my shoulder. I look for tears in his eyes and think I spot the shiny edge of one, like a contact lens.

Well now, I say.

Now we all get up and cry and eat brie and wheat thins. Joanie steps toward me with her husband, William. Until now no one has mentioned God.

I fear for you, Liz. She is crying. I hold her. Why didn't you tell me this before? she murmurs. Oh, Liz, I fear hell for you. What are you doing?

William doesn't bullshit: It's crap, Liz. There's no such thing as an aesthetic suicide. You're not going to be able to stand back afterward and say by jove what a damn good job I did of it. You'll make the *Post,* Liz, not the Whitney. This all smacks of some perverse crypto-Catholic martyrdom of yours. It's deluded. It's a power play.

(I can clear my throat louder than anyone I know.)

I appreciate your candor, William.

You know, he continues, a roomful of people, it sounds beautiful, but it's fishy. Something's not right underneath.

Joanie the star of catechism class: We love you, Liz. God loves you, please—

I understand, I interrupt, if you cannot help me do it.

Help you *do* it? they chorus, horrified. They leave early, forgetting their umbrellas. The room is reeling.

Frank Scherman Franck pulls at his cowlick, sips Cherry Heering. His cowlick bounces back up again, something vaguely lewd. You are a marvel, Liz, he coos. It's a brave and awesome thing you are doing. I never thought you'd actually go through with it, but here you are . . .

(Cherry Heering, Hairy Cherring.) Do you believe in God, Frank Scherman Franck? I ask.

Well, long story, he begins. We have a kind of mutual agreement: I won't believe in him and he won't believe in me. That way no one gets hurt.

Sometimes I still believe in God, Frank Scherman Franck, I say, but then that belief flies away from me like a child on a swing, back and forth, back and forth, and I do not really say this. (Cow lick, lick cow.) I notice William has returned for his umbrella. He stops Elliott in the foyer, says something urgent, something red. I can hear Elliott's reply: If I saw or felt any ambivalence I would, William, but there's no ambivalence. She's sure. She's strong. She knows what she's doing. I have to believe in her.

Excuse me, I say to Frank as I run off to hide temporarily in the bathroom. I lock the door behind me and bury my face in Elliott's bathrobe hanging on the inside hook like a sheepish animal. Hug. Clutch. Press. Cry. I could get lost in it, this vast white country of terrycloth, the terrain of it against my face, Elliott's familiar soapy smells inextricable, filling, spinning my head. I turn around and sink back against the door, against the robe. I do not look in the mirror. This place is a mausoleum of pills and ceramic and fluorescent lights blinking on and off so quickly you think they're on all the time, those clever devils. But we know better don't we. This is where the dead belong, with the dying belonging to the dead belonging to no one. This is not supposed to go like this. I am getting drunk. I think we were supposed to sit around rather politely, perhaps even woodenly, and discuss this thing, cool as iced tea, a parlor of painters and poets like the Paris salons, like television, and we would all agree (my reasoning flawless) that my life ultimately meant my death as well and that it was a right both civil and humane to take whatever actions my free will so determined yadada yadada, and they would pronounce me a genius and not steal the best lines and they would weep just the right amount that anyone should weep for Bastille Day and no one would fucking mention God or hell and when I stepped out of the bathroom I would not see Shennan eyeing Elliott's ass as the two of them stand alone in the kitchen, one slicing cheese, the other arranging crackers, nor would I have to suffer the aphasic stupidity of the articulate (therefore unforgivable) who when offered the topaz necklace of a dying woman do not know what to say (and Myrna, this is not Myrna, Myrna is a poet who flies to Olbia, dismisses lovers, sculpts in words, her poems like the finest diamonds in the finest Fabergés of the finest Czar, not faltering, defeated by topaz). I do not like to watch Myrna grope; she doesn't do it well.

I am something putrid. I wonder if I smell, decaying from the inside out like fruit, yet able to walk among them like the dead among the living, like Christ, for a while, only for a while, until things begin to show, until things become uncomfortable. I return to the living room, grin weakly, stand among my friends. I am something incorrect: a hair in the cottage cheese. Something uncouth: a fart in the elevator.

- - -

Go like this; my husband pushes my head between my knees.

Ugh, what a night, I say, huh.

Ssshhhh. Be quiet. This increases the oxygen to the cortex. You know you're not supposed to drink like that.

I inhale four times with the drama of the first amphibian. How am I doing so far?

The sun is up, depressing me like the mindless smile of a cheerleader. My face is the big bluish-white of white elephants.

The phone rings.

It is Olga, her quiet Slavic cheekbones pale and calming even through the wires, her voice a learned English breathiness affected in the style of too much late night Joan Fontaine. She is sorry, she says, for not having spoken much to me last night. She felt a little bewildered both by my announcement and by the reaction of the others. It was, she says, as if they had already known before and had nothing but clinically prepared affirmations for me, convinced as always of Liz's sound-mindedness.

Well, the dissent left early, I say, and forgot its umbrella.

I, too, am dissenting, she says slowly, like Jane Eyre. Don't the others know what you still have to offer, in terms of your writing, in terms of your daughter?

Olga, I despise people propping my pillows.

Olga is getting cheeky: Perhaps the time has come for you to learn to need people, Liz. And to be patient. You haven't earned your death yet. You want the orgasm without the foreplay.

Look, Olga, at this point I'd take what I could get. Don't get too sexual on me, okay, sweetie? (I can feel myself starting to get mean, my tone invidious.)

Please, Liz. I'm trying to tell you what your sister might have told you. I mean, I couldn't let last night just sit there like that, Shennan standing there like an Indian priestess celebrating death in this fraudulent guise of a philosophy, and Myrna—well, Myrna will be Myrna.

(And sometimes not, I think. God, I'm not in the mood for this. Olga, dear, go back to the moors.)

I care so much for you, Liz, she continues. (Oh, Rochester, take her the fuck away.) It's just that . . . it's like you and your death, you're facing each other like loners from a singles bar who have scarcely spoken. You haven't really kissed or touched and yet are about to plunge into bed together.

(Sex again. Jane Eyre, indeed.)

Honestly, Olga. All this erotica on a Sunday. Has Richard

returned for free piano lessons or something? (I am cruel; a schoolmaster with a switch and a stool.) I really must see what Blaine is shouting about; she's downstairs and has been calling to me for a while now. It may be one of her turtles or something.

Liz, look. I don't want to go like this. Let's have lunch soon.

(We make plans to make plans.)

I think about what William should do.

- - -

Elliott and I have weekly philharmonic seats. I am in bed this Friday, not feeling up to it.

Go ahead, I say. Take Blaine. Take Shennan.

Liz, he drawls, a mild reprimand. He sits at the bed's edge, zooted, smelling of Danish soap, and I think of Ivan Ilych's wife, off to the theater while her husband's kidneys floated in his eyes like cataracts, his legs propped up on the footboard by the manservant—ah, where are the manservants?

Elliott, look at how I'm feeling today. I can't go like this. Please, go ahead without me.

You feel pretty bad, huh, he says, looking at his watch at the same time. He gives me the old honey I'll bring you home a treat, like I'm a fucking retard or something whose nights can be relieved of their hellish sameness with gifts of Colorforms and Sky Bars.

Enjoy, enjoy, you asshole, I do not chirp.

- - -

It is already July. The fireflies will soon be out. My death flashes across my afternoon like a nun in white, hurrying, evanescing, apparitional as the rise of heat off boulevards, the parched white of sails across cement, around the corner, fleeing the sun. I have not yet seen the face, it is hooded, perhaps wrapped, but I know the flow, the cloth of her, moving always in diagonals, in waves toward me, then footlessly away again.

- - -

We told Blaine tonight. We had decided to do it together. We were in the living room.

You're going to die, she said, aren't you? before I had a chance to say, Now you're young and probably don't understand. She has developed a habit of tucking her hair nervously behind her ears when she does not want to cry. She is prophetic. Tuck, tuck.

Yes. And we told her why. And I got a chance, after all, to say you're young and probably don't understand, and she got a chance to look at me with that scrambled gaze of contempt and hurt that only fourth-graders know, and then to close her eyes like an angel and fall into my arms, sobbing, and I sobbed too into that hair tucked behind those ears and I cursed God for this day and Blaine of course wanted to know who would take her to clarinet class.

Tuck, tuck. She lay her head in my lap like a leaky egg. We stayed like that for an hour. I whispered little things to her, smoothing back her hair, about how much I loved her, how patient she would have to be, how strong. At nine-thirty she went silently to her room and lay in bed, swollen-eyed, facing the wall like a spurned and dying lover.

- - -

I realize now what it is that William should do. When the badass wildebeest comes out of the closet and messes up his room, William should blow a trumpet and make the wildebeest cease and desist. He should put his foot down and say, Enough of this darned nonsense, silly wildebeest: Let's get this room picked up! I am practically certain that wildebeests listen to trumpets.

I would tell this to Elliott, but the wildebeest was in the third book. And I finished that long ago.

No, I must think of something else.

- - -

Oh God, it's not supposed to go like this. There I was like Jesus, sure as a blazing rooster, on Palm Sunday riding tall, dauntless as Barbra Streisand, now suddenly on Thursday shoved up against the softer edges of my skin and even Jesus, look, he's crying and whimpering and heaving so, Christ, he pees in his pants, please god, I mean God, don't let me go like this but let me stay right in this garden next to the plastic flamingoes and let me croon the blues till I am crazy with them.

- - -

Elliott has a way of walking in just before dinner and kissing me as if for a publicity shot.

Who do we have out there waiting in the wings, Elliott, fucking Happy Rockefeller? Channel 6 News? Hey, baby, I'm not dead yet; I'm writing, I'm hungry: let's make love, baby, let's do it on the terrace, high and cool, sugar, hey how about the terrace Elliott babydoll, waddaya say?

And if he does not stride angrily from the room, he stays, fumbles insincerely, makes me weep. He has no taste for necrophilia, and I sigh and crave the white of his shoulders under my chin, his breath on my neck, the plum smoothness of him in my hands. And I want it still for me here now as I lie in the blue-black of this aloneness thirsting for love more than I ever thought I could.

- - -

Even at midnight the city groans in the heat. We have had no rain for quite a while. The traffic sounds below ride the night air in waves of trigonometry, the cosine of a siren, the tangent of a sigh, a system, an axis, a logic to this chaos, yes.

- - -

Tomorrow's Bastille Day, Elliott, and I want what I've written for the fourth William book changed. So far William thinks he forgot his umbrella and wanders all over the city looking for it, misfortune following him like an odious dog, until after he is splashed by a truck and nearly hit by a cab, he goes home only to realize he never forgot his umbrella at all. I want that changed. I want him to have all kinds of wonderful, picaresque adventures so that it doesn't even matter if he has lost his umbrella or not. Can you change that for me? Can you think of some wonderful adventures for me? Maybe he meets up with cowboys and a few Indians and has a cookout with music and barbecue beans.

Or meets a pretty little Indian girl and gets married, suggests Elliott, an asshole sometimes, I swear. He doesn't even realize, I guess.

My turn: Yeah, and scalps her and wins hero-of-the-day badge. I guess I'll just have to entrust it all to you, Elliott.

Don't worry, he says, gingerly stroking my hair, which I picture now like the last pieces of thread around a spool.

I really would like to finish it myself, but tomorrow is Bastille Day.

Yes, says Elliott.

•   •   •

Joanie, hon, Joanie with the webbed toes, I know it's late, no, no, don't feel you have to come over, no please don't, Elliott's here, it's fine. I just wanted to say I love you and don't feel sad for me please . . . you know I feel pretty good and these pills, well, they're here in a little saucer staring at me, listen, I'm going to let you go back to bed now and well you know how I've always felt about you Joan and if there is an afterlife . . . yeah well maybe *I'm* not going to heaven, okay . . . what . . . do you think I'm silly? I mean if it wouldn't scare you, maybe I'll try to get in touch, if you wouldn't mind, yes, and please keep an eye out for Blaine for me, Joan, would you, god she's so young and I only just told her about menstruation this past spring and she seemed so interested but then only said, So does that mean all twins look alike? so I know there will be other things she will want to know, you know, and she loves you, Joan, she really does. And be good to Olga for me, I have been so unkind, and remind your husband I've immortalized him, ha! yeah . . . can you believe it, dear rigid soul, and Joanie, take care of yourself and say prayers for me and for Blaine and for Elliott who did cry this morning for the first helpless time, how I do love him, Joan, despite everything

everything I can see from the round eye of this empty saucer, faintly making out a patch of droughted trees and a string of wildebeests, one by one, like the sheep of a child's insomnia, throwing in the towel, circling, lying down in the sun silently to decompose, in spite of themselves, god, there's no music, no trumpet here, it is fast, and there's no sound at all, just this white heat of July going on and on, going on like this

How to Talk
to Your Mother
(Notes)

1982. Without her, for years now, murmur at the defrosting refrigerator, "What?" "Huh?" "Shush now," as it creaks, aches, groans, until the final ice block drops from the ceiling of the freezer like something vanquished.

Dream, and in your dreams babies with the personalities of dachshunds, fat as Macy balloons, float by the treetops.

The first permanent polyurethane heart is surgically implanted.

Someone upstairs is playing "You'll Never Walk Alone" on the recorder. Now it's "Oklahoma!" They must have a Rodgers and Hammerstein book.

1981. On public transportation, mothers with soft, soapy, corduroyed seraphs glance at you, their faces dominoes of compassion. Their seraphs are small and quiet or else restlessly counting bus-seat colors: "Blue-blue-blue, red-red-red, lullow-lullow-lullow." The mothers see you eyeing their children. They smile sympathetically. They believe you envy them. They believe you are childless. They believe they know why. Look quickly away, out the smudge of the window.

1980. The hum, rush, clack of things in the kitchen. These are some of the sounds that organize your life. The clink of the silverware inside the drawer, piled like bones in a mass grave. Your similes grow grim, grow tired.

Reagan is elected President, though you distributed donuts and brochures for Carter.

Date an Italian. He rubs your stomach and says, "These

are marks of stretch, no? Marks of stretch?" and in your dizzy
mind you think: Marks of Harpo, Ideas of Marx, Ides of March,
Beware. He plants kisses on the sloping ramp of your neck, and
you fall asleep against him, your underpants peeled and rolled
around one thigh like a bride's garter.

1979. Once in a while take evening trips past the old unsold
house you grew up in, that haunted rural crossroads two hours
from where you now live. It is like Halloween: the raked, moon-
lit lawn, the mammoth, tumid trees, arms and fingers raised into
the starless wipe of sky like burns, cracks, map rivers. Their black
shadows rock against the side of the east porch. There are dream
shadows, other lives here. Turn the corner slowly but continue
to stare from the car window. This house is embedded in you
deep, something still here you know, you think you know, a
voice at the top of those stairs, perhaps, a figure on the porch,
an odd apron caught high in the twigs, in the too-warm-for-a-
fall-night breeze, something not right, that turret window you
can still see from here, from outside, but which can't be reached
from within. (The ghostly brag of your childhood: "We have
a mystery room. The window shows from the front, but you can't
go in, there's no door. A doctor lived there years ago and gave
secret operations, and now it's blocked off.") The window sits
like a dead eye in the turret.

You see a ghost, something like a spinning statue by a
shrub.

1978. Bury her in the cold south sideyard of that Halloween-
ish house. Your brother and his kids are there. Hug. The min-
ister in a tweed sportscoat, the neighborless fields, the crossroads,
are all like some stark Kansas. There is praying, then someone
shoveling. People walk toward the cars and hug again. Get inside your car with your niece. Wait. Look up through the wind-
shield. In the November sky a wedge of wrens moves south, the
lines of their formation, the very sides and vertices mysteriously

choreographed, shifting, flowing, crossing like a skater's legs. "They'll descend instinctively upon a tree somewhere," you say, "but not for miles yet." You marvel, watch, until, amoeba-slow, they are dark, faraway stitches in the horizon. You do not start the car. The quiet niece next to you finally speaks: "Aunt Ginnie, are we going to the restaurant with the others?" Look at her. Recognize her: nine in a pile parka. Smile and start the car.

1977. She ages, rocks in your rocker, noiseless as wind. The front strands of her white hair dangle yellow at her eyes from too many cigarettes. She smokes even now, her voice husky with phlegm. Sometimes at dinner in your tiny kitchen she will simply stare, rheumy-eyed, at you, then burst into a fit of coughing that racks her small old man's body like a storm.

Stop eating your baked potato. Ask if she is all right.

She will croak: "Do you remember, Ginnie, your father used to say that one day, with these cigarettes, I was going to have to 'face the mucus'?" At this she chuckles, chokes, gasps again.

Make her stand up.

Lean her against you.

Slap her lightly on the curved mound of her back.

Ask her for chrissakes to stop smoking.

She will smile and say: "For chrissakes? Is that any way to talk to your mother?"

At night go in and check on her. She lies there awake, her lips apart, open and drying. Bring her some juice. She murmurs, "Thank you, honey." Her mouth smells, swells like a grave.

1976. The Bicentennial. In the laundromat, you wait for the time on your coins to run out. Through the porthole of the dryer, you watch your bedeviled towels and sheets leap and fall. The radio station piped in from the ceiling plays slow, sad

Motown; it encircles you with the desperate hopefulness of a boy at a dance, and it makes you cry. When you get back to your apartment, dump everything on your bed. Your mother is knitting crookedly: red, white, and blue. Kiss her hello. Say: "Sure was warm in that place." She will seem not to hear you.

1975. Attend poetry readings alone at the local library. Find you don't really listen well. Stare at your crossed thighs. Think about your mother. Sometimes you confuse her with the first man you ever loved, who ever loved you, who buried his head in the pills of your sweater and said magnificent things like "Oh god, oh god," who loved you unconditionally, terrifically, like a mother.

The poet loses his nerve for a second, a red flush through his neck and ears, but he regains his composure. When he is finished, people clap. There is wine and cheese.

Leave alone, walk home alone. The downtown streets are corridors of light holding you, holding you, past the church, past the community center. March, like Stella Dallas, spine straight, through the melodrama of street lamps, phone posts, toward the green house past Borealis Avenue, toward the rear apartment with the tilt and the squash on the stove.

Your horoscope says: Be kind, be brief.

You are pregnant again. Decide what you must do.

1974. She will have bouts with a mad sort of senility. She calls you at work. "There's no food here! Help me! I'm starving!" although you just bought forty dollars' worth of groceries yesterday. "Mom, there is too food there!"

When you get home the refrigerator is mostly empty. "Mom, where did you put all the milk and cheese and stuff?" Your mother stares at you from where she is sitting in front of the TV set. She has tears leaking out of her eyes. "There's no food here, Ginnie."

There is a rustling, scratching noise in the dishwasher. You open it up, and the eyes of a small rodent glint back at you. It scrambles out, off to the baseboards behind the refrigerator. Your mother, apparently, has put all the groceries inside the dishwasher. The milk is spilled, a white pool against blue, and things like cheese and bologna and apples have been nibbled at.

1973. At a party when a woman tells you where she bought some wonderful pair of shoes, say that you believe shopping for clothes is like masturbation—everyone does it, but it isn't very interesting and therefore should be done alone, in an embarrassed fashion, and never be the topic of party conversation. The woman will tighten her lips and eyebrows and say, "Oh, I suppose you have something more fascinating to talk about." Grow clumsy and uneasy. Say, "No," and head for the ginger ale. Tell the person next to you that your insides feel sort of sinking and vinyl like a Claes Oldenburg toilet. They will say, "Oh?" and point out that the print on your dress is one of paisleys impregnating paisleys. Pour yourself more ginger ale.

1972. Nixon wins by a landslide.

Sometimes your mother calls you by her sister's name. Say, "No, Mom, it's me. Virginia." Learn to repeat things. Learn that you have a way of knowing each other which somehow slips out and beyond the ways you have of not knowing each other at all.

Make apple crisp for the first time.

1971. Go for long walks to get away from her. Walk through wooded areas; there is a life there you have forgotten. The smells and sounds seem sudden, unchanged, exact, the papery crunch of the leaves, the mouldering sachet of the mud. The trees are crooked as backs, the fence posts splintered, trusting and precarious in their solid grasp of arms, the asters spindly, dry, white,

havishammed (Havishammed!) by frost. Find a beautiful red-
dish stone and bring it home for your mother. Kiss her. Say:
"This is for you." She grasps it and smiles. "You were always
such a sensitive child," she says.
    Say: "Yeah, I know."

1970. You are pregnant again. Try to decide what you should do.
Get your hair chopped, short as a boy's.

1969. Mankind leaps upon the moon.
    Disposable diapers are first sold in supermarkets.
    Have occasional affairs with absurd, silly men who tell you
to grow your hair to your waist and who, when you are sad,
tickle your ribs to cheer you up. Moonlight through the blinds
stripes you like zebras. You laugh. You never marry.

1968. Do not resent her. Think about the situation, for instance, when you take the last trash bag from its box: you must
throw out the box by putting it in that very trash bag. What was
once contained, now must contain. The container, then, becomes
the contained, the enveloped, the held. Find more and more that
you like to muse over things like this.

1967. Your mother is sick and comes to live with you. There
is no place else for her to go. You feel many different emptinesses.
    The first successful heart transplant is performed in South
Africa.

1966. You confuse lovers, mix up who had what scar, what
car, what mother.

1965. Smoke marijuana. Try to figure out what has made your
life go wrong. It is like trying to figure out what is stinking up
the refrigerator. It could be anything. The lid off the mayon-
naise, Uncle Ron's honey wine four years in the left corner.

Broccoli yellowing, flowering fast. They are all metaphors. They are all problems. Your horoscope says: Speak gently to a loved one.

1964. Your mother calls long distance and asks whether you are coming home for Thanksgiving, your brother and the baby will be there. Make excuses.

"As a mother gets older," your mother says, "these sorts of holidays become increasingly important."

Say: "I'm sorry, Mom."

1963. Wake up one morning with a man you had thought you'd spend your life with, and realize, a rock in your gut, that you don't even like him. Spend a weepy afternoon in his bathroom, not coming out when he knocks. You can no longer trust your affections. People and places you think you love may be people and places you hate.

Kennedy is shot.

Someone invents a temporary artificial heart, for use during operations.

1962. Eat Chinese food for the first time, with a lawyer from California. He will show you how to hold the chopsticks. He will pat your leg. Attack his profession. Ask him whether he feels the law makes large spokes out of the short stakes of men.

1961. Grandma Moses dies.

You are a zoo of insecurities. You take to putting brandy in your morning coffee and to falling in love too easily. You have an abortion.

1960. There is money from your father's will and his life insurance. You buy a car and a green velvet dress you don't need. You drive two hours to meet your mother for lunch on Saturdays. She suggests things for you to write about, things she's heard on the radio: a woman with telepathic twins, a woman with no feet.

1959. At the funeral she says: "He had his problems, but he was a generous man," though you know he was tight as a scout knot, couldn't listen to anyone, the only time you remember loving him being that once when he got the punchline of one of your jokes before your mom did and looked up from his science journal and guffawed loud as a giant, the two of you, for one split moment, communing like angels in the middle of that room, in that warm, shared light of mind.

Say: "He was okay."

"You shouldn't be bitter," your mother snaps. "He financed you and your brother's college educations." She buttons her coat. "He was also the first man to isolate a particular isotope of helium, I forget the name, but he should have won the Nobel Prize." She dabs at her nose.

Say: "Yeah, Mom."

1958. At your brother's wedding, your father is taken away in an ambulance. A tiny cousin whispers loudly to her mother, "Did Uncle Will have a hard attack?" For seven straight days say things to your mother like: "I'm sure it'll be okay," and "I'll stay here, why don't you go home and get some sleep."

1957. Dance the calypso with boys from a different college. Get looped on New York State burgundy, lose your virginity, and buy one of the first portable electric typewriters.

1956. Tell your mother about all the books you are reading at college. This will please her.

1955. Do a paint-by-numbers of Elvis Presley. Tell your mother you are in love with him. She will shake her head.

1954. Shoplift a cashmere sweater.

1953. Smoke a cigarette with Hillary Swedelson. Tell each other your crushes. Become blood sisters.

1952. When your mother asks you if there are any nice boys in junior high, ask her how on earth would you ever know, having to come in at nine! every night. Her eyebrows will lift like theater curtains. "You poor, abused thing," she will say.

Say, "Don't I know it," and slam the door.

1951. Your mother tells you about menstruation. The following day you promptly menstruate, your body only waiting for permission, for a signal. You wake up in the morning and feel embarrassed.

1949. You learn how to blow gum bubbles and to add negative numbers.

1947. The Dead Sea Scrolls are discovered.

You have seen too many Hollywood musicals. You have seen too many people singing in public places and you assume you can do it, too. Practice. Your teacher asks you a question. You warble back: "The answer to number two is twelve." Most of the class laughs at you, though some stare, eyes jewel-still, fascinated. At home your mother asks you to dust your dresser. Work up a vibrato you could drive a truck through. Sing: "Why do I have to do it now?" and tap your way through the dining room. Your mother requests that you calm down and go take a nap. Shout: "You don't care about me! You don't care about me at all!"

1946. Your brother plays "Shoofly Pie" all day long on the Victrola.

Ask your mother if you can go to Ellen's for supper. She will say, "Go ask your father," and you, pulling at your fingers, walk out to the living room and whimper by his chair. He is reading. Tap his arm. "Dad? Daddy? Dad?" He continues reading his science journal. Pull harder on your fingers and run back to the kitchen to tell your mother, who storms into the living room, saying, "Why don't you ever listen to your children when they try to talk to you?" You hear them arguing. Press your face into a kitchen towel, ashamed, the hum of the refrigerator motor, the drip in the sink scaring you.

1945. Your father comes home from his war work. He gives you a piggyback ride around the broad yellow thatch of your yard, the dead window in the turret, dark as a wound, watching you. He gives you wordless pushes on the swing.

Your brother has new friends, acts older and distant, even while you wait for the school bus together.

You spend too much time alone. You tell your mother that when you grow up you will bring your babies to Australia to see the kangaroos.

Forty thousand people are killed in Nagasaki.

1944. Dress and cuddle a tiny babydoll you have named "the Sue." Bring her everywhere. Get lost in the Wilson Creek fruit market, and call softly, "Mom, where are you?" Watch other children picking grapes, but never dare yourself. Your eyes are small, dark throats, your hand clutches the Sue.

1943. Ask your mother about babies. Have her read to you only the stories about babies. Ask her if she is going to have a baby. Ask her about the baby that died. Cry into her arm.

1940. Clutch her hair in your fist. Rub it against your cheek.

1939. As through a helix, as through an ear, it is here you are nearer the dream flashes, the other lives.

There is a tent of legs, a sundering of selves, as you both gasp blindly for breath. Across the bright and cold, she knows it when you try to talk to her, though this is something you never really manage to understand.

Germany invades Poland.

The year's big song is "Three Little Fishies" and someone, somewhere, is playing it.

Amahl and the Night Visitors: A Guide to the Tenor of Love

11/30. Understand that your cat is a whore and can't help you. She takes on love with the whiskery adjustments of a gold-digger. She is a gorgeous nomad, an unfriend. Recall how just last month when you got her from Bob downstairs, after Bob had become suddenly allergic, she leaped into your lap and purred, guttural as a German chanteuse, familiar and furry as a mold. And Bob, visibly heartbroken, still in the room, sneezing and giving instructions, hoping for one last cat nuzzle, descended to his hands and knees and jiggled his fingers in the shag. The cat only blinked. For you, however, she smiled, gave a fish-breath peep, and settled.

"Oh, well," said Bob, getting up off the floor. "Now I'm just a thing of her kittenish past."

That's the way with Bob. He'll say to the cat, "You be a good girl now, honey," and then just shrug, go back downstairs to his apartment, play jagged, creepy jazz, drink wine, stare out at the wintry scalp of the mountain.

12/1. Moss Watson, the man you truly love like no other, is singing December 23 in the Owonta Opera production of *Amahl and the Night Visitors.* He's playing Kaspar, the partially deaf Wise Man. Wisdom, says Moss, arrives in all forms. And you think, Yes, sometimes as a king and sometimes as a hesitant phone call that says the king'll be late at rehearsal don't wait up, and then when you call back to tell him to be careful not to let the cat out when he comes home, you discover there's been no rehearsal there at all.

At three o'clock in the morning you hear his car in the

driveway, the thud of the front door. When he comes into the bedroom, you see his huge height framed for a minute in the doorway, his hair lit bright as curry. When he stoops to take off his shoes, it is as if some small piece of his back has given way, allowing him this one slow bend. He is quiet. When he gets into bed he kisses one of your shoulders, then pulls the covers up to his chin. He knows you're awake. "I'm tired," he announces softly, to ward you off when you roll toward him. Say: "You didn't let the cat out, did you?"

He says no, but he probably should have. "You're turning into a cat mom. Cats, Trudy, are the worst sort of surrogates."

Tell him you've always wanted to run off and join the surrogates.

Tell him you love him.

Tell him you know he didn't have rehearsal tonight.

"We decided to hold rehearsal at the Montessori school, what are you now, *my* mother?"

In the dark, discern the fine hook of his nose. Smooth the hair off his forehead. Say: "I love you Moss are you having an affair with a sheep?" You saw a movie once where a man was having an affair with a sheep, and acted, with his girlfriend, the way Moss now acts with you: exhausted.

Moss's eyes close. "I'm a king, not a shepherd, remember? You're acting like my ex-wife."

His ex-wife is now an anchorwoman in Missouri.

"Are you having a regular affair? Like with a person?"

"Trudy," he sighs, turns away from you, taking more than his share of blanket. "You've got to stop this." Know you are being silly. Any second now he will turn and press against you, reassure you with kisses, tell you oh how much he loves you. "How on earth, Trudy," is what he finally says, "would I ever have the time for an affair?"

12/2. Your cat is growing, eats huge and sloppy as a race-horse. Bob named her Stardust Sweetheart, a bit much even for

Bob, so you and Moss think up other names for her: Pudge, Pudgemuffin, Pooch, Poopster, Secretariat, Stephanie, Emily. Call her all of them. "She has to learn how to deal with confusion," says Moss. "And we've gotta start letting her outside." Say: "No. She's still too little. Something could happen." Pick her up and away from Moss. Bring her into the bathroom with you. Hold her up to the mirror. Say: "Whossat? Whossat pretty kitty?" Wonder if you could turn into Bob.

12/3. Sometimes Moss has to rehearse in the living room. King Kaspar has a large black jewelry box about which he must sing to the young, enthralled Amahl. He must open drawers and haul out beads, licorice, magic stones. The drawers, however, keep jamming when they're not supposed to. Moss finally tears off his fake beard and screams, "I can't do this shit! I can't sing about money and gewgaws. I'm the tenor of love!" Last year they'd done *La Bohème* and Moss had been Rodolfo.

This is the sort of thing he needs you for: to help him with his box. Kneel down beside him. Show him how one of the drawers is off its runner. Show him how to pull it out just so far. He smiles and thanks you in his berserk King Kaspar voice: "Oh, thank you, thank you, thank you!" He begins his aria again: " 'This is my box. This is my box. I never travel without my box.' "

All singing is, says Moss, is sculpted howling.

Say, "Bye." Wheel the TV into the kitchen. Watch MacNeil-Lehrer. Worry about Congress.

Listen to the goose-call of trains, all night, trundling by your house.

12/4. Sometimes the phone rings, but then the caller hangs up.

12/5. Your cat now sticks her paws right in the water dish while she drinks, then steps out from her short wade and licks them, washes her face with them, repeatedly, over the ears and down, like an itch. Take to observing her. On her feet the gray and pink configurations of pads and fur look like tiny baboon faces. She sees you watching, freezes, blinks at you, then busies herself again, her face in her belly, one leg up at a time, an intent ballerina in a hairy body stocking. And yet she's growing so quickly, she's clumsy. She'll walk along and suddenly her hip will fly out of whack and she'll stop and look at it, not comprehending. Or her feet will stumble, or it's difficult for her to move her new bulk along the edges of furniture, her body pushing itself out into the world before she's really ready. It puts a dent in her confidence. She looks at you inquiringly: *What is happening to me?* She rubs against your ankles and bleats. You pick her up, tuck her under your chin, your teeth clenched in love, your voice cooey, gooey with maternity, you say things like, "How's my little dirt-nose, my little fuzz-face, my little honey-head?"

"Jesus, Trudy," Moss yells from the next room. "Listen to how you talk to that cat."

12/6. Though the Christmas shopping season is under way, the store you work at downtown, Owonta Flair, is not doing well. "The malls," groans Morgan, your boss. "Every Christmas the malls! We're doomed. These candy cane slippers. What am I gonna do with these?"

Tell her to put one slipper from each pair in the window along with a mammoth sign that says, MATES INSIDE. "People only see the sign. Thom McAn did it once. They got hordes."

"You're depressed," says Morgan.

12/7. You and Moss invite the principals, except Amahl, over to dinner one night before a rehearsal. You also invite Bob. Three kings, Amahl's unwed mother, you, and Bob: this way four people can tell cranky anecdotes about the production, and two people can listen.

"This really is a trashy opera," says Sonia, who plays Amahl's mother. "Sentimental as all get-out." Sonia is everything you've always wanted to be: smart, Jewish, friendly, full-haired as Easter basket grass. She speaks with a mouthful of your spinach pie. She says she likes it. When she has swallowed, a piece of spinach remains behind, wrapped like a gap around one of her front teeth. Other than that she is very beautiful. Nobody says anything about the spinach on her tooth.

Two rooms away the cat is playing with a marble in the empty bathtub. This is one of her favorite games. She bats the marble and it speeds around the porcelain like a stock car. The noise is rattley, continuous.

"What is that weird noise?" asks Sonia.

"It's the beast," says Moss. "We should put her outside, Trudy." He pours Sonia more wine, and she murmurs, "Thanks."

Jump up. Say: "I'll go take the marble away."

Behind you you can hear Bob: "She used to be mine. Her name is Stardust Sweetheart. I got allergic."

Melchior shouts after you: "Aw, leave the cat alone, Trudy. Let her have some fun." But you go into the bathroom and take the marble away anyhow. Your cat looks up at you from the tub, her head cocked to one side, sweet and puzzled as a child movie star. Then she turns and bats drips from the faucet. Scratch the scruff of her neck. Close the door when you leave. Put the marble in your pocket.

You can hear Balthazar making jokes about the opera. He calls it *Amyl and the Nitrates.*

"I've always found Menotti insipid," Melchior is saying when you return to the dining room.

"Written for NBC, what can you expect," Sonia says. Soon she is off raving about *La Bohème* and other operas. She uses words like *verismo, messa di voce,* Montserrat Caballe. She smiles. "An opera should be like contraception: about *sex, not* children."

Start clearing the plates. Tell people to keep their forks

for dessert. Tell them that no matter what anyone says, you think *Amahl* is a beautiful opera and that the ending, when the mother sends her son off with the kings, always makes you cry. Moss gives you a wink. Get brave. Give your head a toss. Add: "Papage*no,* Papage*na*—to me, *La Bohème*'s just a lot of scarves."

There is some gulping of wine.

Only Bob looks at you and smiles. "Here. I'll help you with the plates," he says.

Moss stands and makes a diversionary announcement: "Sonia, you've got a piece of spinach on your tooth."

"Christ," she says, and her tongue tunnels beneath her lip like an elegant gopher.

12/8. Sometimes still Moss likes to take candlelight showers with you. You usually have ten minutes before the hot water runs out. Soap his back, the wide moguls of his shoulders registering in you like a hunger. Press yourself against him. Whisper: "I really do like *La Bohème,* you know."

"It's okay," Moss says, all forgiveness. He turns and grabs your buttocks.

"It's just that your friends make me nervous. Maybe it's work, Morgan that forty-watt hysteric making me crazy." Actually you like Morgan.

Begin to hum a Dionne Warwick song, then grow self-conscious and stop. Moss doesn't like to sing in the shower. He has his operas, his church jobs, his weddings and bar mitzvahs— in the shower he is strictly off-duty. Say: "I mean, it *could* be Morgan."

Moss raises his head up under the spray, beatific, absent. His hair slicks back, like a baby's or a gangster's, dark with water, shiny as a record album. "Does Bob make you nervous?" he asks.

"Bob? Bob suffers from terminal sweetness. I like Bob."

"So do I. He's a real gem."

Say: "Yeah, he's a real chum."

"I said *gem*," says Moss. "Not *chum*." Things fall quiet. Lately you've been mishearing each other. Last night in bed you said, "Moss, I usually don't like discussing sex, but—" And he said, "I don't like disgusting sex either." And then he fell asleep, his snores scratching in the dark like zombies.

Take turns rinsing. Don't tell him he's hogging the water. Ask finally, "Do you think Bob's gay?"

"Of course he's gay."

"How do you know?"

"Oh, I don't know. He hangs out at Sammy's in the mall."

"Is that a gay bar?"

"Bit of everything." Moss shrugs.

Think: Bit of everything. Just like a mall. "Have you ever been there?" Scrub vigorously between your breasts.

"A few times," says Moss, the water growing cooler.

Say: "Oh." Then turn off the faucet, step out onto the bath mat. Hand Moss a towel. "I guess because I work trying to revive our poor struggling downtown I don't get out to these places much."

"I guess not," says Moss, candle shadows wobbling on the shower curtain.

12/9. Two years ago when Moss first moved in, there was something exciting about getting up in the morning. You would rise, dress, and, knowing your lover was asleep in your bed, drive out into the early morning office and factory traffic, feeling that you possessed all things, Your Man, like a Patsy Cline song, at home beneath your covers, pumping blood through your day like a heart.

Now you have a morbid fascination with news shows. You get up, dress, flick on the TV, sit in front of it with a bowl of cereal in your lap, quietly curse all governments everywhere, get into your car, drive to work, wonder how the sun has the nerve to show its face, wonder why the world seems to be picking up speed, even old ladies pass you on the highway, why you don't have a single erotic fantasy that Moss isn't in, whether there really are such things as vitamins, and how would you rather die cancer or a car accident, the man you love, at home, asleep, like a heavy, heavy heart through your day.

"Goddamn slippers," says Morgan at work.

12/10. The cat now likes to climb into the bathtub and stand under the dripping faucet in order to clean herself. She lets the water bead up on her face, then wipes herself, neatly dislodging the gunk from her eyes.

"Isn't she wonderful?" you ask Moss.

"Yeah. Come here you little scumbucket," he says, slapping the cat on the haunches, as if she were a dog.

"She's not a dog, Moss. She's a cat."

"That's right. She's a cat. Remember that, Trudy."

12/11. The phone again. The ringing and hanging up.

12/12. Moss is still getting in very late. He goes about the business of fondling you, like someone very tired at night having to put out the trash and bolt-lock the door.

He sleeps with his arms folded behind his head, elbows protruding, treacherous as daggers, like the enemy chariot in *Ben-Hur.*

12/13. Buy a Christmas tree, decorations, a stand, and lug them home to assemble for Moss. Show him your surprise.

"Why are the lights all in a clump in the back?" he asks, closing the front door behind him.

Say: "I know. Aren't they great? Wait till you see me do the tinsel." Place handfuls of silver icicles, matted together like alfalfa sprouts, at the end of all the branches.

"Very cute," says Moss, kissing you, then letting go. Follow him into the bathroom. Ask how rehearsal went. He points to the kitty litter and sings: " 'This is my box. I never travel without my box.' "

Say: "You are not a well man, Moss." Play with his belt loops.

12/14. The white fur around the cat's neck is growing and looks like a stiff Jacobean collar. "A rabato," says Moss, who suddenly seems to know these things. "When are we going to let her go outside?"

"Someday when she's older." The cat has lately taken to the front window the way a hypochondriac takes to a bed. When she's there she's more interested in the cars, the burled fingers of the trees, the occasional squirrel, the train tracks like long fallen ladders, than she is in you. Call her: "Here pootchy-kootchy-honey." Ply her, bribe her with food.

12/15. There are movies in town: one about Brazil, and one about sexual abandonment in upstate New York. "What do you say, Moss. Wanna go to the movies this weekend?"

"I can't," says Moss. "You know how busy I am."

12/16. The evening news is full of death: young marines, young mothers, young children. By comparison you have already lived forever. In a kind of heaven.

12/17. Give your cat a potato and let her dribble it about soccer-style. She's getting more coordinated, conducts little dramas with the potato, pretends to have conquered it, strolls over it, then somersaults back after it again. She's not bombing around, crashing into the sideboards anymore. She's learning moves. She watches the potato by the dresser leg, stalks it, then pounces. When she gets bored she climbs up onto the sill and looks out, tail switching. Other cats have spotted her now, have started coming around at night. Though she will want to go, do not let her out the front door.

12/18. The phone rings. You say hello, and the caller hangs up. Two minutes later it rings again, only this time Moss answers it in the next room, speaks softly, cryptically, not the hearty phone voice of the Moss of yesteryear. When he hangs up, wander in and say, blasé as paste, "So, who was that?"

"Stop," says Moss. "Just stop."

Ask him what's the big deal, it was Sonia wasn't it.

"Stop," says Moss. "You're being my wife. Things are repeating themselves."

Say that nothing repeats itself. Nothing, nothing, nothing. "Sonia, right?"

"Trudy, you've got to stop this. You've been listening to too much *Tosca.* I'm going out to get a hamburger. Do you want anything?"

Say: "I'm the only person in the whole world who knows you, Moss. And I don't know you at all anymore."

"That's a different opera," he says. "I'm going out to get a hamburger. Do you want anything?"

Do not cry. Stick to monosyllables. Say: "No. Fine. Go."

Say: "Please don't let the cat out."

Say: "You should wear a hat it's cold."

12/19. Actually what you've been listening to is Dionne Warwick's Golden Hits—musical open heart surgery enough for you. Sometimes you pick up the cat and waltz her around, her purr staticky and intermittent as a walkie-talkie.

On "Do You Know the Way to San Jose," you put her down, do an unfortunate charleston, while she attacks your stockinged feet, thinking them large rodents.

Sometimes you knock into the Christmas tree.

Sometimes you collapse into a chair and convince yourself that things are still okay.

When Robert MacNeil talks about mounting inflation, you imagine him checking into a motel room with a life-size, blow-up doll. This is, once in a while, how you amuse yourself.

When Moss gets in at four in the morning, whisper: "There are lots of people in this world, Moss, but you can't be in love with them all."

"I'm not," he says, "in love with the mall."

12/20. The mall stores stay open late this last week before Christmas. Moss is supposed to be there, "in the gazebo next to the Santa gazebo," for an *Amahl and the Night Visitors* promotional. Decide to drive up there. Perhaps you can look around in the men's shops for a sweater for Moss, perhaps even one for Bob as well. Last year was a bad Christmas: you and Moss returned each other's gifts for cash. You want to do better this year. You want to buy: sweaters.

The mall parking lot, even at 7 p.m., is, as Moss would say, packed as a bag, though you do manage to find a space.

Inside the mall entranceway it smells of stale popcorn, dry heat, and three-day-old hobo urine. A drunk, slumped by the door, smiles and toasts you with nothing.

Say: "Cheers."

To make your journey down to the gazebos at the other end of the mall, first duck into all the single-item shops along the way. Compare prices with the prices at Owonta Flair: things are a little cheaper here. Buy stuff, mostly for Moss and the cat.

In the pet food store the cashier hands you your bagged purchase, smiles, and says, "Merry Christmas."

Say: "You, too."

In the men's sweater shop the cashier hands you your bagged purchase, smiles, and says, "Merry Christmas."

Say: "You, too."

In the belt shop the cashier hands you your bagged purchase, smiles, and says, "Come again."

Say: "You, too." Grow warm. Narrow your eyes to seeds.

In the gazebo next to the Santa gazebo there is only an older
man in gray coveralls stacking some folding chairs.

Say: "Excuse me, wasn't *Amahl and the Night Visitors*
supposed to be here?"

The man stops for a moment. "There's visitors," he says,
pointing out and around, past the gazebo to all the shoppers.
Shoppers in parkas. Shoppers moving slow as winter. Shoppers
who haven't seen a crosswalk or a window in hours.

"I mean the opera promotional."

"The singers?" He looks at his watch. "They packed it in
a while ago."

Say thank you, and wander over to Cinema 1-2-3 to read
the movie posters. It's when you turn to go that you see Moss
and Bob coming out together from the bar by the theater. They
look tired.

Adjust your packages. Walk over. Say: "Hi. I guess I missed
the promo, so I was thinking of going to a movie."

"We ended it early," says Moss. "Sonia wasn't feeling well.
Bob and I just went into Sammy's for a drink."

Look and see the sign that, of course, reads SAMMY'S.

Bob smiles and says, "Hello, Trudy." Because Bob says
hello and never *hi,* he always manages to sound a little like Mister Rogers.

You can see some of Moss's makeup and glue lines. His
fake beard is sticking out from his coat pocket. Smile. Say: "Well,
Moss. Here all along I thought it was Sonia, and it's really Bob."
Chuck him under the chin. Keep your smile steady. You are the
only one smiling. Not even Bob. You have clearly said the wrong
thing.

"Fuck off, Trudy," Moss says finally, palming his hair back off his forehead.

Bob squirms in his coat. "I believe I forgot something," he says. "I'll see you both later." And he touches Moss's arm, turns, disappears back inside Sammy's.

"Jesus Christ, Trudy." Moss's voice suddenly booms through the mall. You can see a few stores closing up, men coming out to lower the metal night gates. Santa Claus has gotten down from the gazebo and is eating an egg roll.

Moss turns from you, charges toward the exit, an angry giant with a beard sticking out of his coat pocket. Run after him and grab his sleeve, make him stop. Say: "I'm sorry, Moss. What am I doing? Tell me. What am I doing wrong?" You look up at his face, with the orange and brown lines and the glue patches, and realize: He doesn't understand you've planned your lives together. That you have even planned your deaths together, not really deaths at all but more like a *pas de deux*. Like Gene Kelly and Leslie Caron in *An American in Paris,* only older.

"You just won't let people be," says Moss, each consonant spit like a fish bone.

Say: "People be? I don't understand. Moss, what is happening to us?" You want to help him, rescue him, build houses and magnificent lawns around him.

"To *us?*"

Moss's voice is loud. He puts on his gloves. He tells you you are a child. He needs to get away. For him you have managed to reduce love, like weather, to a map and a girl, and he needs to get away from you, live someplace else for a while, and think.

The bag with the cat food slips and falls. "The opera's in three days, Moss. Where are you going to go?"

"Right now," he says, "I'm going to get a hamburger." And he storms toward the mall doors, pushes against all of them until he finds the one that's open.

Stare and mumble at the theater candy concession. "Good and Plenty. There's no Good and Plenty." Your bangs droop into your vision. You keep hearing "Jingle Bells," over and over.

In the downtown theaters of your childhood, everything was made of carved wood, and in the ladies' rooms there were framed photographs of Elizabeth Taylor and Ava Gardner. The theaters had names: The Rialto, The Paramount. There were ushers and Good and Plenty. Ushers with flashlights and bow ties. That's the difference now. No ushers. Now you have to do everything by yourself.

"Trudy," says a voice behind you. "Would you like to be accompanied to the movies?" The passive voice. It's Bob's. Turn to look at him, but as with the Good and Plenty, you don't really see, everything around you vague and blurry as glop in your eye.

Say: "Sure. Why not."

In Cinema 3, sit in seats close to the aisle. Listen to the Muzak. The air smells like airplane air.

"It's a strange thing about Moss," Bob is saying, looking straight ahead. "He's so busy with the opera, it pushes him up against certain things. He ends up feeling restless and smothered. But, Trudy, Moss is a good man. He really is."

Don't say anything, and then say, finally, "Moss who?"

Stare at the curtain with the rose-tinted lights on it. Try to concentrate on more important matters, things like acid rain.

Bob taps his fingers on the metal arm of the seat. Say: "Look, Bob. I'm no idiot. I was born in New York City. I lived there until I was four. Come on. Tell me: Who's Moss sleeping with?"

"As far as I know," says Bob, sure and serious as a tested hypothesis, "Moss isn't sleeping with anyone."

Continue staring at the rose lights. Then say in a loud contralto: "He's sleeping with *me*, Bob. That's who he's sleeping with."

When the lights dim and the curtains part, there arrive little cigarette lighters on the screen telling you not to smoke. Then there are coming attractions. Bob leans toward you, says, "These previews are horrible."

Say: "Yeah. Nothing Coming Soon."

There are so many previews you forget what movie you've come to see. When the feature presentation comes on, it takes you by surprise. The images melt together like a headache. The movie seems to be about a woman whose lover, losing interest in her, has begun to do inexplicable things like yell about the cat, and throw scenes in shopping malls.

"What is this movie about?"

"Brazil," whispers Bob.

The audience has begun to laugh at something someone is doing; you are tense with comic exile. Whisper: "Bob, I'm gonna go. Wanna go?"

"Yes, in fact, I do," says Bob.

It's ten-thirty and cold. The mall stores are finally closed. In the parking lot, cars are leaving. Say to Bob: "God, look how many people shop here." The whole world suddenly seems to you like a downtown dying slow.

Spot your car and begin to head toward it. Bob catches your sleeve. "My car's the other way. Listen. Trudy. About Moss: No matter what's going on with him, no matter what he decides he has to do, the man loves you. I know he does."

Gently pull your sleeve away. Take a step sideways toward your car. Headlights, everywhere headlights and tires crunching. Say: "Bob, you're a sweet person. But you're sentimental as all get-out." Turn on the nail of your boot and walk.

At home the cat refuses to dance to Dionne Warwick with you. She sits on the sill of the window, rumbling in her throat, her tail a pendulum of fluff. Outside, undoubtedly, there are suitors, begging her not to be so cold-hearted. "Ya got friends

out there?" When you turn off the stereo, she jumps down from
the sill and snakes lovingly about your ankles. Say something
you never thought you'd say. Say: "Wanna go out?" She looks
at you, all hope and supplication, and follows you to the door,
carefully watching your hand as it moves for the knob: she wants
you to let her go, to let her go and be. Begin slowly, turn, pull.
The suction of door and frame gives way, and the cold night
insinuates itself like a kind of future. She doesn't leave immediately. But her whole body is electrified, surveying the yard for
eyes and rustles, and just to the left of the streetlight she suddenly spots them—four, five, phosphorescent glints—and, without a nudge, without ever looking back, she scurries out, off the
porch, down after, into some sweet unknown, some somehow
known unknown, some yet very old religion.

12/21. Every adoration is seasonal as Christmas.

Moss stops by to get some things. He's staying with Balthazar for a few days, then after the opera and Christmas and
all, he'll look for an efficiency somewhere.

Nod. "Efficiency. Great. That's what hell is: efficient." You
want to ask him if this is all some silly opera where he's leaving
in order to spare you his tragic, bluish death by consumption.

He says, "It's just something I've got to do." He opens
cupboards in the kitchen, closets in the hallway, pulls down
boxes, cups, boots. He is slow about it, doesn't do it in a mean
way, you are grateful for that.

"What have you been doing tonight?" he asks, not looking,
but his voice is urgent as a touch.

"I watched two hours of MacNeil-Lehrer. You can get it
on channel seven and then later on channel four."

"Right," says Moss. "I know."

Pause. Then say: "Last night I let the cat out. Finally."

Moss looks at you and smiles.

Smile back and shrug, as if all the world were a comedy

you were only just now appreciating. Moss begins to put a hand to your shoulder but then takes it back. "Congratulations, Trudy," he murmurs.

"But she hasn't come back yet. I haven't seen her since last night."

"She'll come back," says Moss. "It's only been a day."

"But it's been a whole day. Maybe I should put in ads."

"It's only been one day. She'll come back. You'll see."

Step away from him. Outside, in front of the streetlight, something like snow is falling. Think back again to MacNeil-Lehrer. Say in a level tone: "You know, there are people who know more about it than we do, who say that there is no circumnavigating a nuclear war, we will certainly have one, it's just a matter of time. And when it happens, it's going to dissolve all our communications systems, melt silicon chips—"

"Trudy, please." He wants you to stop. He knows this edge in your voice, this MacNeil-Lehrer edge. All of the world knotted and failing on your tongue.

"And then if you're off living someplace else, in some efficiency, how will I be able to get in touch with you? There I'll be, Moss, all alone in my pink pom-pom slippers, the entire planet exploding all around, and I won't be able to talk to you, to say—" In fifth grade you learned the first words ever spoken on the telephone: *Mr. Watson, come here, I want you.* And suddenly, as you look at him, at the potatoey fists of his cheeks, at his broom-blonde hair, it hits you as it would a child: Someday, like everybody, this man you truly love like no other is going to die. No matter how much you love him, you cannot save him. No matter how much you love: nothing, no one, lasts.

"Moss, we're not safe."

And though there's no flutter of walls, or heave of the floor, above the frayed-as-panic rug, shoes move, and Moss seems to come unstuck, to float toward you, his features beginning to slide in downward diagonals, some chip in his back dissolving, allowing him to bend. His arms reach out to bring you close to his chest. The buttons of his shirt poke against you, and his chin hooks, locks around your neck. When he is gone, the world will grow dull as Mars.

"It's okay," he whispers, his lips moving against your hair. Things grow fuzzy around the edge like a less than brilliant lie. "It's okay," says Moss.

How to Become
a Writer

First, try to be something, anything, else. A movie star/astronaut. A movie star/missionary. A movie star/kindergarten teacher. President of the World. Fail miserably. It is best if you fail at an early age—say, fourteen. Early, critical disillusionment is necessary so that at fifteen you can write long haiku sequences about thwarted desire. It is a pond, a cherry blossom, a wind brushing against sparrow wing leaving for mountain. Count the syllables. Show it to your mom. She is tough and practical. She has a son in Vietnam and a husband who may be having an affair. She believes in wearing brown because it hides spots. She'll look briefly at your writing, then back up at you with a face blank as a donut. She'll say: "How about emptying the dishwasher?" Look away. Shove the forks in the fork drawer. Accidentally break one of the freebie gas station glasses. This is the required pain and suffering. This is only for starters.

In your high school English class only at Mr. Killian's face. Decide faces are important. Write a villanelle about pores. Struggle. Write a sonnet. Count the syllables: nine, ten, eleven, thirteen. Decide to experiment with fiction. Here you don't have to count syllables. Write a short story about an elderly man and woman who accidentally shoot each other in the head, the result of an inexplicable malfunction of a shotgun which appears mysteriously in their living room one night. Give it to Mr. Killian as your final project. When you get it back, he has written on it: "Some of your images are quite nice, but you have no sense of plot." When you are home, in the privacy of your own room, faintly scrawl in pencil beneath his black-inked comments: "Plots are for dead people, pore-face."

Take all the babysitting jobs you can get. You are great
with kids. They love you. You tell them stories about old people
who die idiot deaths. You sing them songs like "Blue Bells of
Scotland," which is their favorite. And when they are in their
pajamas and have finally stopped pinching each other, when they
are fast asleep, you read every sex manual in the house, and
wonder how on earth anyone could ever do those things with
someone they truly loved. Fall asleep in a chair reading Mr.
McMurphy's *Playboy*. When the McMurphys come home, they
will tap you on the shoulder, look at the magazine in your lap,
and grin. You will want to die. They will ask you if Tracey took
her medicine all right. Explain, yes, she did, that you promised
her a story if she would take it like a big girl and that seemed
to work out just fine. "Oh, marvelous," they will exclaim.

Try to smile proudly.

Apply to college as a child psychology major.

As a child psychology major, you have some electives.
You've always liked birds. Sign up for something called "The
Ornithological Field Trip." It meets Tuesdays and Thursdays at
two. When you arrive at Room 134 on the first day of class,
everyone is sitting around a seminar table talking about metaphors. You've heard of these. After a short, excruciating while,
raise your hand and say diffidently, "Excuse me, isn't this Bird-
watching One-oh-one?" The class stops and turns to look at you.
They seem to all have one face—giant and blank as a vandalized
clock. Someone with a beard booms out, "No, this is Creative
Writing." Say: "Oh—right," as if perhaps you knew all along.
Look down at your schedule. Wonder how the hell you ended
up here. The computer, apparently, has made an error. You start
to get up to leave and then don't. The lines at the registrar this
week are huge. Perhaps you should stick with this mistake. Perhaps your creative writing isn't all that bad. Perhaps it is fate.

Perhaps this is what your dad meant when he said, "It's the age of computers, Francie, it's the age of computers."

Decide that you like college life. In your dorm you meet many nice people. Some are smarter than you. And some, you notice, are dumber than you. You will continue, unfortunately, to view the world in exactly these terms for the rest of your life.

The assignment this week in creative writing is to narrate a violent happening. Turn in a story about driving with your Uncle Gordon and another one about two old people who are accidentally electrocuted when they go to turn on a badly wired desk lamp. The teacher will hand them back to you with comments: "Much of your writing is smooth and energetic. You have, however, a ludicrous notion of plot." Write another story about a man and a woman who, in the very first paragraph, have their lower torsos accidentally blitzed away by dynamite. In the second paragraph, with the insurance money, they buy a frozen yogurt stand together. There are six more paragraphs. You read the whole thing out loud in class. No one likes it. They say your sense of plot is outrageous and incompetent. After class someone asks you if you are crazy.

Decide that perhaps you should stick to comedies. Start dating someone who is funny, someone who has what in high school you called a "really great sense of humor" and what now your creative writing class calls "self-contempt giving rise to comic form." Write down all of his jokes, but don't tell him you are doing this. Make up anagrams of his old girlfriend's name and name all of your socially handicapped characters with them. Tell him his old girlfriend is in all of your stories and then watch how funny he can be, see what a really great sense of humor he can have.

Your child psychology advisor tells you you are neglecting courses in your major. What you spend the most time on should be what you're majoring in. Say yes, you understand.

In creative writing seminars over the next two years, everyone continues to smoke cigarettes and ask the same things: "But does it work?" "Why should we care about this character?" "Have you earned this cliché?" These seem like important questions.

On days when it is your turn, you look at the class hopefully as they scour your mimeographs for a plot. They look back up at you, drag deeply, and then smile in a sweet sort of way.

You spend too much time slouched and demoralized. Your boyfriend suggests bicycling. Your roommate suggests a new boyfriend. You are said to be self-mutilating and losing weight, but you continue writing. The only happiness you have is writing something new, in the middle of the night, armpits damp, heart pounding, something no one has yet seen. You have only those brief, fragile, untested moments of exhilaration when you know: you are a genius. Understand what you must do. Switch majors. The kids in your nursery project will be disappointed, but you have a calling, an urge, a delusion, an unfortunate habit. You have, as your mother would say, fallen in with a bad crowd.

Why write? Where does writing come from? These are questions to ask yourself. They are like: Where does dust come from? Or: Why is there war? Or: If there's a God, then why is my brother now a cripple?

These are questions that you keep in your wallet, like calling cards. These are questions, your creative writing teacher says, that are good to address in your journals but rarely in your fiction.

The writing professor this fall is stressing the Power of the Imagination. Which means he doesn't want long descriptive stories about your camping trip last July. He wants you to start in a realistic context but then to alter it. Like recombinant DNA. He wants you to let your imagination sail, to let it grow big-bellied in the wind. This is a quote from Shakespeare.

Tell your roommate your great idea, your great exercise of imaginative power: a transformation of Melville to contemporary life. It will be about monomania and the fish-eat-fish world of life insurance in Rochester, New York. The first line will be "Call me Fishmeal," and it will feature a menopausal suburban husband named Richard, who because he is so depressed all the time is called "Mopey Dick" by his witty wife Elaine. Say to your roommate: "Mopey Dick, get it?" Your roommate looks at you, her face blank as a large Kleenex. She comes up to you, like a buddy, and puts an arm around your burdened shoulders. "Listen, Francie," she says, slow as speech therapy. "Let's go out and get a big beer."

The seminar doesn't like this one either. You suspect they are beginning to feel sorry for you. They say: "You have to think about what is happening. Where is the story here?"

The next semester the writing professor is obsessed with writing from personal experience. You must write from what you know, from what has happened to you. He wants deaths, he wants camping trips. Think about what has happened to you. In three years there have been three things: you lost your virginity; your parents got divorced; and your brother came home from a forest ten miles from the Cambodian border with only half a thigh, a permanent smirk nestled into one corner of his mouth.

About the first you write: "It created a new space, which hurt and cried in a voice that wasn't mine, 'I'm not the same anymore, but I'll be okay.' "

About the second you write an elaborate story of an old married couple who stumble upon an unknown land mine in their kitchen and accidentally blow themselves up. You call it: "For Better or for Liverwurst."

About the last you write nothing. There are no words for this. Your typewriter hums. You can find no words.

At undergraduate cocktail parties, people say, "Oh, you write? What do you write about?" Your roommate, who has consumed too much wine, too little cheese, and no crackers at all, blurts: "Oh, my god, she always writes about her dumb boyfriend."

Later on in life you will learn that writers are merely open, helpless texts with no real understanding of what they have written and therefore must half-believe anything and every-thing that is said of them. You, however, have not yet reached this stage of literary criticism. You stiffen and say, "I do not," the same way you said it when someone in the fourth grade accused you of really liking oboe lessons and your parents really weren't just making you take them.

Insist you are not very interested in any one subject at all, that you are interested in the music of language, that you are interested in—in—syllables, because they are the atoms of poetry, the cells of the mind, the breath of the soul. Begin to feel woozy. Stare into your plastic wine cup.

"Syllables?" you will hear someone ask, voice trailing off, as they glide slowly toward the reassuring white of the dip.

Begin to wonder what you do write about. Or if you have anything to say. Or if there even is such a thing as a thing to say. Limit these thoughts to no more than ten minutes a day; like sit-ups, they can make you thin.

You will read somewhere that all writing has to do with one's genitals. Don't dwell on this. It will make you nervous.

Your mother will come visit you. She will look at the cir-cles under your eyes and hand you a brown book with a brown briefcase on the cover. It is entitled: *How to Become a Business Executive.* She has also brought the *Names for Baby* encyclopedia you asked for; one of your characters, the aging clown–schoolteacher, needs a new name. Your mother will shake her head and say: "Francie, Francie, remember when you were going to be a child psychology major?"

Say: "Mom, I like to write."

She'll say: "Sure you like to write. Of course. Sure you like to write."

Write a story about a confused music student and title it: "Schubert Was the One with the Glasses, Right?" It's not a big hit, although your roommate likes the part where the two violinists accidentally blow themselves up in a recital room. "I went out with a violinist once," she says, snapping her gum.

Thank god you are taking other courses. You can find sanctuary in nineteenth-century ontological snags and invertebrate courting rituals. Certain globular mollusks have what is called "Sex by the Arm." The male octopus, for instance, loses the end of one arm when placing it inside the female body during intercourse. Marine biologists call it "Seven Heaven." Be glad you know these things. Be glad you are not just a writer. Apply to law school.

From here on in, many things can happen. But the main one will be this: you decide not to go to law school after all, and, instead, you spend a good, big chunk of your adult life telling people how you decided not to go to law school after all. Somehow you end up writing again. Perhaps you go to graduate school. Perhaps you work odd jobs and take writing courses at night. Perhaps you are working on a novel and writing down all the clever remarks and intimate personal confessions you hear during the day. Perhaps you are losing your pals, your acquaintances, your balance.

You have broken up with your boyfriend. You now go out with men who, instead of whispering "I love you," shout: "Do it to me, baby." This is good for your writing.

Sooner or later you have a finished manuscript more or less. People look at it in a vaguely troubled sort of way and say, "I'll bet becoming a writer was always a fantasy of yours, wasn't it?" Your lips dry to salt. Say that of all the fantasies possible in the world, you can't imagine being a writer even making the top twenty. Tell them you were going to be a child psychology major. "I bet," they always sigh, "you'd be great with kids." Scowl fiercely. Tell them you're a walking blade.

Quit classes. Quit jobs. Cash in old savings bonds. Now you have time like warts on your hands. Slowly copy all of your friends' addresses into a new address book.

Vacuum. Chew cough drops. Keep a folder full of fragments.

An eyelid darkening sideways.

World as conspiracy.

Possible plot? A woman gets on a bus.

Suppose you threw a love affair and nobody came.

At home drink a lot of coffee. At Howard Johnson's order the cole slaw. Consider how it looks like the soggy confetti of a map: where you've been, where you're going—"You Are Here," says the red star on the back of the menu.

Occasionally a date with a face blank as a sheet of paper asks you whether writers often become discouraged. Say that sometimes they do and sometimes they do. Say it's a lot like having polio.

"Interesting," smiles your date, and then he looks down at his arm hairs and starts to smooth them, all, always, in the same direction.

To Fill

There is no dignity in appetites. That blanched pathetic look at salad bars, those scramblers for some endless consumption I am no exception. I was raised on Ward's catalogs god those toys and shorts sets everything, everything, wonderfully turquoise. I moaned for the large black olives of restaurants, the fancy chunky dressings. I pined like a toad at gumball machines. And now, at thirty-five, I have stolen money, for no other reason than this nameless, bullying ache. A blistery rash has crept up out of my mouth, red and slick, making my face look vaguely genital, out of control. I have a recent tic at the eye, at the outer corner, something fluttering, trying to scamper away.

My mother has convinced herself she is physically and mentally ill and has checked into St. Veronica's, although the doctors don't know what to do with her. With my stolen money I buy her things, I buy me things. In stores, in front of nuns, embarrassingly, I twitch and perspire with a sort of jazz, an improvised rhythm, unpredictable, hungry.

In the cool arterial corridors of St. Veronica's, doors swing open and shut, open and shut like valves. I am big, an over-weight, natural dirt blonde with a nervous rash and think some-how this will keep nuns from harassing me I am a bit afraid of them. Out of deference, I wear a bra and no eyeshadow.

As I pass Sister Mary Marian at reception I nod and smile and then feel my face contort: the stench is worse than yesterday, an acrid medley of something like ether and old cantaloupe good god Mother how can you stand it here.

I am intent on getting her out. I have brought her a new Chinese cookbook and a wok and carry them wrapped in orange paper in a huge box in front of me. Yesterday I brought her a deep violet evening gown. You have a whole life ahead of you, I said, holding it up and dancing it around, and she stared at me acidly from her pillow, unblinking, quietly chewing gum.

Again today I head for the swinging doors. Open and shut. That's what the store detectives will say good god I must really stop this. Excuse me, I say to a brigade of wheelchairers trundling by, groggy and pale with mobile IV's. Excuse me oh god pardon me. I am awkward in the elevator. Everywhere there are nuns. I am not Catholic, but I have been to too many Baptist potlucks.

My mother sits up briskly, unsmiling. Now, what the devil is this? she asks. She has been lying on her back, clipping coupons from the *Inquirer,* a good sign, practicality.

How are you feeling today, Mother? I set the wok down by her bed. My eye begins to fidget.

What the devil is this now? she asks again. Another gift?

Ma, I just wanted you to see—

Can't keep these things here, Riva, she interrupts curtly. Can't keep all these things.

Well bring them home, Ma. Come on. You really don't need to be in this hospital anymore. The doctors all agree. It's up to you.

She looks away, then with scissors begins retrimming the coupons more closely along the dotted lines. Slivers of newsprint fall to her sheets. She says nothing.

Look, I say, if you don't want to go back to your apartment, you can come stay with Tom and me for a few weeks or so. I pause.

She stops cutting, glares up at me, and scowls: Who is this Tom guy anyway?

Tom, my husband of six years, has lately been a frequent casualty of her feigned senility. Mother, I say calmly. Tom has been my husband for six years, now you know that, and I wish you would just cut all of this out.

At this she grows especially dotty and waves her scissors at me, making little snips in the air.

You don't need to be here, I sniff, unconvinced. Besides, it smells in this place.

The scissors freeze solemnly, dramatically, in front of her face.

Riva, that's no way to talk about a good Catholic hospital. She looks away again, histrionic. I hate it, I hate it when she does this.

Whatever happened to that Phillip someone you were seeing all those years why, she sighs, we thought for sure you'd settle down and have us over for fondue on Thursdays my he was a sweet boy.

I cannot, cannot go through this again. Not today. I grab my bag and start for the door. When did my mother become such a loon?

There's a great recipe for Garlic Snow Peas in there, I say. You should take a look. A silver-toothed redhead who also shares the room, whips back her bed curtain, grins, and blows me a kiss good-bye. Gaga. They're all gaga here. My mother is shouting after me: Damn it who is this Tom guy anyway? Two nuns arrive, always, always in pairs, to calm her down.

I drive home. I drive the car home and think of you, Phil, faraway and invisible, even my mother speaking of you, as does this sad ache, thoughts of you, you are thoughts, springing up everywhere. The French for plateful *also means state of mind— you wrote that on a postcard from Provence. I have it in a box somewhere. O Riva, you are a woman of whims and cravings, you said that of me, calling me expansive. You live, you said, you live from the twinges in your hips.*

I have stolen money. I have stolen money from the Leigenbaum's department store where I am manager of Scarves and Handbags. I do it with the returns. The inventory count is always clumsy, so I can take one return on a bag or scarf and double it, there are perforated receipts for both, and I can make the amount of the return and still refund the customer his money. The registers come out even, the books balance. I often stay late and alone to make sure. In a week I can make from two hundred to four hundred dollars, depending on the returns, depending on the twinges in my hips. It has been three weeks now. Ever since Mardi Gras. No one knows. I get ravenous. I buy things.

Tom is in insurance. He also likes to buy policies for himself. We have many, many policies. I have three lifes and two autos. He has four lifes, two autos, two fire and thefts, three hospital and accidents, and two mutilated limb and/or organs. One eye equals three right fingers and a thumb, says the policy. We also have something yellow with a diamond and fur clause. We sleep well at night. Unless it is raining or we've had a fight or Jeffrey is sick—then we toss like dinghies.

Why is Tom looking at me funny this evening does he suspect?

He says: How was work?

I say: Fine. How about you?

He says: Fine. Baker's coming in from Pittsburgh tomorrow to discuss the sectional meeting.

I say: Well, that will be nice. Shall I expect him for dinner?

He says: Nah, 'sgotta fly back right away. We'll grab something in Center City.

I say: Fine.

He says: What's bugging Jeffrey? Is it nursery school?

I say: I think it's his dancing class. No big deal. He's just getting behind or lost or something.

He says: Is that what his teacher told you?

I say: No, Jeffrey mentioned it. For no reason I add: He's a good honest kid.

He says: Well, what's the problem? Has he missed classes or what?

I say: Look, he's just a little frustrated trying to remember some of the steps. I really think that's all it is.

He says: Hell, why's a kid his age gotta take a goddamn pre-school dance class, anyway?

And I say: Because it's a fucking international law, why do you think?

And that's when Tom calls me hostile and says I've been snapping at him for weeks and I say, look, he's your son and if you don't encourage him early in some sort of meaningful aesthetic endeavor, he'll end up on the streets killing hubcaps and stealing prostitutes and Tom smiles slightly and says don't you have that backwards and I say Tom sometimes you really just miss the point of life sometimes you are an inexpressibly hollow, hollow man, you don't know a damn about what's important in this world and that's when he looks at me aghast and I realize I have sprung a leak somewhere and as he calls Riva please come back here I run upstairs to the bay window and hide behind my new floor-length half-silk drapes I bought just last week with the money, the money, breathing into the smooth seamless backing they smell new, new, because I really don't know myself now what it is I'm talking about, but it must be something, this jittery pang, this space, this hole must have a name I wonder what it is who is this Tom guy anyway?

A dream. A dream is like a church, cool and dark and wood and brass, the jeweled jelly-jar windows a place to scurry into from off the street in the night I dreamed of you, Phil. You stood before me and undressed, then sinking into me nuzzling with the perfect bone of your chin, the perfect O of your mouth, humming to the Bruckner or the Mahler, I didn't know, it was a name that made me think of the Bronx, and your face beneath me, close and closed and traveling briefly opened, smiling up at me, huge trembling me, and whispered: Oh the largeness.

How we loved each other with forks.

The woman in the health food store I believe is slowly losing her mind. Every time I go in there she is slumped on the wooden stool behind the register more dazed, more sad than before. She recognizes me less. Today I am the only one in there and when I say excuse me, can I get two pounds of bulgar wheat, she continues to stare at the coconut shampoos, her legs frozen and crossed, her back a curved mound beneath the same pink-gray sweater she drapes like a small cape over her shoulders. Finally she says huh but never looks up.

Bulgar wheat? I say gently. Coarse? Like last week?

Yeah. She pulls at the sweater, then goes through some sort of pelvic swivel which tilts the stool just enough to spill her down and out of it. She scuffs around the counter to the bulgar wheat, reaches for a scoop, a paper bag, and then bursts into sobs. I try to think of what to do. I quickly grab three coconut shampoos to help out her business a little and then go to her, put my arm around her, and tell her about Tom's secret affair last year in Scranton and how I visited him there as a surprise and learned of the whole thing and got drunk and stuck postage stamps all over myself and tried to mail myself home, that always cheers people up when I tell it in Scarves and Handbags. She smiles, shuffles over to the register, charges me for four not three coconut shampoos and the bulgar wheat.

I walk toward the car.

A basset hound caroms dizzily up the sidewalk ahead of me, peeing on everything.

Today I am taking Jeffrey alias Batman to visit my mother. Although he is officially too young to visit, he has won Sister Mary Marian's heart by asking her if she were his fairy godmother and she, quite enthralled with this idea, now lies incorrigibly, telling everyone that he's regulation exempt, it's fine he can go in. These are the kind of nuns I like.

Mother places the chocolate Last Supper I have paid twenty

dollars for disinterestedly at the foot of the bed and reaches jubilantly for Jeffrey. Come see Gramma, she sings.

Hi Gramma, he chirps obediently and climbs up into her arms in his cape and mask, he is such a good kid. There are so many funny fairies here at your house, Gramma, he continues.

My mother shifts her feet uncomfortably beneath the covers and the Last Supper cracks onto the floor.

Well, Jeffrey dear, have you been well?

Jeffrey's head does two full expressionless bobs.

Mother tosses a look at me which for some reason seems to say: How did you and this Tom ever manage such a lovely child?

She continues: How do you like going to nursery school, Jeffrey?

Jeffrey looks at her with sudden interest, his eyes behind his mask wide as soft-boiled eggs. He pauses, then warbles: Back and forth, back and forth.

Tell Gramma, Jeffrey, what the strange clothes are that you have on today.

I'm Batman, says Jeffrey.

You're Batman?! squeals my delighted mother.

Yup, he says, and shapes his fingers into a gun and pulls the trigger, blowing off her face. Bang, he says.

She is startled. Now Jeffrey dear, you don't mean that, she coos nervously, taking his little hand and gently, quietly, returning it to his lap. It flies back up with a fierce quickness. Jeffrey looks at her face, her sour-breath face, and doesn't smile. Bang, he says again from behind the mask, the finger curling slowly, firmly. Bang.

You love once, I told you. Even when you love over and over again it is the same once, the same one. And you sent me your recipes—Ezra Pound Cake, Beef Mallarmé—and you wrote: Do you think if you eat one meal, every meal after that is the

same meal, just because it too is a meal? And I said some are the
same meal.

In the hospital cafeteria Jeffrey asks me if he can have a
BB gun. He is eating around the crusts of his bologna sandwich,
pulling out the lettuce and dropping it unsurreptitiously onto
the floor.

Of course not, I say. Take your mask off while you're eating. He obeys.

Why on earth do you want a BB gun?

He shrugs his shoulders. I dunno, he says and I can hear
his legs swinging beneath the table, his sneakers hitting the
aluminum, vibrating his Jello-O. Dad'll let me.

No, he won't, Jeffrey, now that's the end of it.

He thinks about this for a while. Can I have some ice
cream, then?

No. Finish your sandwich.

Can I . . . (now he's just thinking up any old thing) . . .
take this home with me? He holds up a plastic fork.

Good god. All right.

Goody, he says.

Tuesday at work I have to yell at Amahara. She has mis-
priced all the Italian clutches.

Big deal, bubbleass, she mutters into her own right
shoulder.

One more crack like that, Amahara, and you're through.

I didn't say nothing, she protests, wickedly wide-eyed.

Just watch it. My voice is scraping, ugly, it unnerves me.
I go back out on the floor and re-mark the bags myself. It is a
thankless, mechanical chore, tag after tag, one after another.
The Italian clutches have brassy leering clasps and I can see
myself in them, muzzy and sickeningly golden. I am suddenly
embarrassed to be marking up such flimsy merchandise.

I leave early not even checking the afternoon's returns, pick up Batman from nursery school, drive home, and lying in bed later ask Tom if he thinks I have a big ass like a bubble and he says no.

When I'm working at the store, Jeffrey stays at Mr. Fernandez's nursery school on Spruce Street. He is a former aging hippie who became a panhandler outside the art museum where I met him, years ago, when I was trying to get pregnant. He thought I was Tricia Nixon and vociferously demanded a quarter. When I failed to drop one into his coffee can because I was looking at a brochure on Cézanne's *The Great Bathers,* he started hissing things at me.

Excuse me? I said, stopping on the stairs to look at him. I was disoriented after so much post-impressionism. And then he knew, glancing up at me, that he had it all wrong. Too big, he said. Too big. I'm sorry. I thought you were Tricia Nixon. And that's when he got up and walked over to me, a dusky, swaying man, and said in a slight accent: Geeze lady, I'm really sorry. He extended his right hand and I shook it, putting away the brochure, and then we talked a bit, he about the eighteenth-century Chippendale commode in the English wing, and I about him, asking what he was doing with his life, why he was here. He merely smiled sadly, I suppose the truest sort of explanation he could muster, and said what he would really like to do is raise a family and how envious he was of me, still young and newly pregnant and—

And I said: Pregnant? What makes you say that? (Sometimes I am sensitive about my size.)

And then he became even more apologetic and said, well, that it was just a way he had, a witchiness, but not a bad witchiness, and he just knew these things.

And sure enough eight months later Batman flew out, and Mr. Fernandez, newly scrubbed and reformed, the beneficiary of ten thousand dollars from a dead Ohio cousin and of manicure advice from me, threw a giant shower and gave me a yellow horse pinata never to be whacked open but simply to hang in Jeffrey's room, a lesson in hope and greed and peaceful coexistence, and it has been there ever since. And Mr. Fernandez has successfully opened a nursery school on Spruce Street called Pinata Pre-School, and only I, not even Tom, know of his museum-step past and I have promised not to divulge it, and he has hugged me gratefully on several occasions and we have become quite close friends and he is really so good, so good with children.

Amahara and I had drinks at lunch today. I guess we are on speaking terms again. We sent to La Kommissary and she told me about a guy she went out with this weekend.

He's not interested in what's inside, complains Amahara. I want a guy who wants my heart, you know? I want him to look for my heart.

You know when he's fumbling with your breasts? I flutter my eyes at Amahara. He's looking for your heart. They all do that.

What a bitter hag I have become.

Amahara grins. He's really into orange.

But what does that mean, into orange?

Like really into it. She smiles enigmatically.

The color?

Yeah. Really into it.

But what do you mean? His car? His hair? Your hair?

His life, she says dramatically. He's really into it.

Into it, I repeat dumbly, believing I am trying to under-stand; what is wrong with me, I thought we were on speaking terms, what are speaking terms am I on them with anyone am I from outer space, is she?

I can't believe, I say firmly, hoping it will pass, that a person could be so into it.

For damn sure, says Amahara.

I pick up the check. Amahara goes for her wallet, but I say nope, it's on me, I'm into it.

Intuit, you said, blowing out the candle. Intuition is the secret life of fat cells. And then you burrowed into me, whispering your questions.

I am becoming hugely depressed. Like last year. Just a month ago I was better, sporting a simpler, terse sort of disenchantment, a neat black vest of sadness. Elegant ironies leaped from my mouth fine as *cuisses de grenouilles.* Now the darkness sleeps and wakes in me daily like an Asian carnivore at the Philly zoo.

In my little white house I am in a slump. I look around. All these possessions, all these new things, are little teeth, death markers, my home one compact little memorial park remember when they used to be called cemeteries. Now even gravestones are called family monuments, like these things, monuments to the family. I stare at my gold faucets, my new chairs, my popcorn popper, and my outsized spice rack—thyme leaves, time leaves—and wonder how they got here, how I have arrived at this point of clutter. These things, things, things, my mind is shouting and I hurl appliances, earrings, wine glasses, into the kitchen trash and, gripped immediately by a zinging, many-knuckled panic, pick them out again, hurry, hurry, one by one, rinse them off, put them back away, behind their doors, watch TV, breathe, watch TV.

My face worsens, and my eye, yet Tom doesn't seem to notice. It seems my question about my ass, however, has made him a bit braver, and he suggests, gently, as we lie side by side in the dark, ever so delicately, that perhaps I should lose some —Christ in the foothills, Riva, why don't you lose some— weight.

He has another business trip to Scranton on Thursday, he says. Won't be back until late Saturday.

Scranton. History dangles in front of me, a terrible mobile. My arms cannot move. My forehead opens up like a garage door. You've got to be kidding, I gasp, panicked.

No, why? he murmurs. Shouldn't be too bad.

Oh come off it, Tom. These suburban, marital clichés. They've crawled into us like tapeworms. Put a sugar cube on the tongue, flash a light up the ass, and they poke out their tiny white heads to investigate, they're eating us Tom there's something eating us.

He snorts, smooths his baggy pajamas, closes his handsome eyes. He says he doesn't understand why it is always late at night that I grow so incomprehensible.

I grow so incomprehensible.

I am stealing more and more money. I keep it in my top drawer beneath my underwear, along with my diaphragm and my lipstick and my switchblade these are things a woman needs.

You are the man removing my bobby pins, my hair unfurling, the one who saunters in still, grinning then absconding with all of my pulses, over and over again, that long graceful stride toward a city, toward a bathroom, toward a door. I sleep alone this week, my husband gone, rolling into my own empty arms might they be yours, sleep on top of them as if to kill them, and in the morning they are dead as salamis until I massage the blood down into them again with my palm. Sweet, sweet Riva, you said to the blind white place behind my ear. Come live with me and be my lunch.

After I've picked up Jeffrey and the two of us have come home, we are alone in the kitchen and he teaches me what he has learned in his dance class.

Shooba plié, shooba plié, he chants, hanging on to the Formica edge of the counter, jiggling and squatting repeatedly in his corduroys. He always looks so awkward I'm sure he's doing something wrong.

What's a shooba? I inquire, silly me.

It's this, he says, doing lord knows what with his pelvis. Then you make a Driveway, he explains, indicating the newly created space between his turned-out feet, but you don't drive in it, he adds.

You mean, it's just for show? I ask, incredulous. My smile frustrates him.

Welp . . . Mommy, listen! You just do Jellyfish fingers, hang, hang, then leapareeno! and he grand jetés, or sort of, across the linoleum, whoops loudly, slides into the potato cabinet. Then he's up again, his fallen socks now bunched at his instep, and he scoots across the floor with little brush steps, singing hoo-la, hoo-la, brock-co-lee!

How did he get this far from me? So short a time and already he is off and away, inventing his own life. I want to come up behind him, cover his head with my dirty, oniony apron, suck him back up into my body I want to know his bones again, to keep him from the world.

Mommy?

My brain feels crammed and gassy as if with cole slaw. You live, I read once, you live if you dance to the voice that ails you.

You go like this, Mom.

I stop my staring. Like this? I am no dummy. I am swiftly up on my toes, flitting past the refrigerator, my arms flapping like sick ducks. Hoo-la, hoo-la, I sing. Hoo-la-la.

Sometimes I find myself walking down the street or through Scarves and Handbags thinking about absolutely nothing, my mind worrying its own emptiness. I think: Everyone is thinking bigger thoughts than I, everyone is thinking thoughts. Sometimes it scares me, this bone box of a head of mine, this clean, shiny ashtray.

And when after one hundred years, I am reading to Jeffrey, a prince came across Sleeping Beauty in the forest and kissed her, she awoke with a start and said, Prince! What took you so long? for she had been asleep for quite some time and all of her dreams were in reruns.

Jeffrey gulps solemnly: Like Starsky and Hutch.

And then the prince took Sleeping Beauty in his arms and said: Let us be married, fair lady, and we shall live happily ever after or until the AFC championship games, whichever comes first.

Ma-om! Jeffrey lets out a two-toned groan. That's not how it goes.

Oh, excuse me, I apologize. You're right. He says: Let us be married, fair dozing one. And I shall make you my princess. And Sleeping Beauty says: Oh, handsome prince. I love you so. But I have been asleep for a hundred years and am old enough to be your grandmother.

Jeffrey giggles.

The prince thought about this and was just about to say, Well, that being the case maybe I'll be running along now, when a magic bluebird swooped down out of the sky and made him one hundred years older as well, and then boy did Sleeping Beauty have a good laugh.

Did they live happily ever after?

Gee, honey, you know it just doesn't say. What do you think?

Yup, says Jeffrey, not smiling.

Knock, knock, says Mr. Fernandez.

Who's there? I smile, on my way home with Jeffrey. I am double-parked on Spruce Street.

Amnesia.
Amnesia who?

The moon is full is serene, wanders indolent and pale as a cow, a moon cow through my window, taking me to its breast, swaddling me in its folds of light. I leave on this moon, float out into the night on it, wash out like a wave and encircle the earth, I move with a husbandless gait, an ease about the flanks, the luminous hugeness of milk at my eyes I shift, disappear by slow degrees, travel, looking. Where did you go?

I owe. I owe the store so much money I cannot believe it. I let Amahara go home early today and then go into the back office, get the books out again, and calculate how much it has been: so much I cannot say.

At least I have done it neatly. There is something soothing in arithmetic, in little piles, little stacks of numbers that obey you.

Tuesday I stop at Wanamaker's and pick up ruby-colored satin slippers for my mother and walk out of the store without paying for them. I then head for Mr. Fernandez's to pick up Jeffrey. Together, big blonde, little blonde, we walk the sixteen blocks to St. Veronica's, no need to get home early; Tom's still in Scranton.

Sister Mary Marian is ecstatic at seeing Jeffrey again. He gives her a big juicy kiss on the cheek and she giggles and reddens. It makes me uncomfortable.

In the elevator I touch my face, touch my eyes to see if they are behaving, if they are being, if they are having, or misbehaving, miss being had. The words conflate and dizzy me, smack of the errors of my life I misbe. I mishave. Jeffrey pulls on my arm as if he wants to tell me something. We are stalled on the third floor while two orderlies wheel in a giant cart of medical supplies, glasses, and linens. I bend down so Jeffrey can whisper whatever it is he wants to say, and with both his hands he begins assiduously smoothing my hair back and out of the way. When he has the space around my ear sufficiently cleared, however, he doesn't say anything, but just presses his face close against my head.

Jeffrey, hon, what is it? The doors now shut and we resume our ascent.

Nothing, he whispers loudly.

Nothing? I ask, thinking he might be scared of something. I am still bent over.

I just wanted to look at your ear, he explains.

We walk in dully, not knowing what to expect. We leave our raincoats on.

Mother seems to be having a good day, her spirits up gliding around the white metal room greeting the world like pleasant hosts. And we are the parasites that have just trudged sixteen blocks, the pair of sights, the parricides.

Riva, dear, and Jeffrey. I was hoping you would come today. How's Tom?

But I think she's said who's Tom and I freeze, very tired, not wanting to get into that again.

Do you feel all better, Gramma? Jeffrey asks with a yawn, climbing on the metal footboard, looking as if purposefully at the meaningless clipboard there.

Gramma just has to speak to the doctor before she can leave here, she says.

I am shocked that my mother is talking about leaving. Does she no longer think of herself as mad? As Catholic? I look at her face and it is smiling, softened like ice cream.

Mother, do you mean that? Will you come home with us? I feel equivocal and liver-lipped.

We'll see, she says, has forever said, as I sometimes do now to Jeffrey. And yet it seems more hopeful, more certain. I feel, however, the slow creep of ambivalence in me: How will she behave, will she insist on refrying the pork chops, will she snore unforgivably from the den?

Ladies always say that, announces my clever son. He has now wandered over to the window and stands tiptoe, just barely able to peer out at the emergency entrance in the wing directly opposite this one. Wow, he shouts. Ampulnses. Neato.

Mother, I think it would be great for you to leave here, and as I've said before, we would love to have you. I sit at the bed squeezing her hand, having no idea what I really want her to do, astounded at my disingenuousness—would she just watch TV nice and quiet all day on the couch?

Jeffrey is still watching things out the window, saying: They take sick people for rides, right Gramma?

I haven't been able to stop eating. Amahara remarks today when I put three Lifesavers in my mouth at once: Boy, don't you know it's Lent? You haven't stopped eating for weeks. Silence. Have you?

I am reminded of a man's coat I bought once at a used clothing store, a store of dead people's clothes, and how I found an old Lifesaver in the pocket and popped it in my mouth, a dead man's candy. You'll eat anything, won't you, said Tom.

I am suddenly angry at Amahara. I march out wordlessly, straightening my spine. I stand next to Mrs. Rosenbaum our best charge customer and recommend the Korean paisleys while every cell in my body grumbles and gossips. Later I do a small operation with the Ann Klein receipts in the back. I will buy a new dishwasher.

I steal back into dreams of you, your unmade bed a huge open-faced sandwich. I lie back against you, fit the crook of your arm around my neck and into the curve at the base of my skull, bring your hand around to meet my mouth, chewing on your fingers, one by one, as a child might, listening to you tell stories.

Once upon a time I was in a strange position regarding women, you begin. I saw myself, as someone once said of Mohammed Ali, as a sort of pelvic missionary.

Ah, I murmur. The pelvic missionary position.

And your calluses press against my lips and teeth and your fingers strum my smile like a harp I am yours, yours, despite your stories I am yours.

I want to diet. I want to slink. I want to slink in a mink at the sink.

Batman is giving me dance lessons again before dinner. Glide, glide, goom-bah, he says, his lithe little body cutting S-weaves across the floor. Mom, he sighs, feigning exasperation at my swivel-hipped attempt to do what he is doing. He is imperious, in imitation of his teacher, a frustrated bursitic Frenchman named Oleg. Move just your feet. Everything else will follow. Goom-bah!

Do I grow slinky? I think of carrot sticks and ice and follow Jeffrey's lead. I am snapping my fingers, wiggling, bumping, grinding. Mom, giggles Jeffrey. That's too kinky.

And later, alone, the night outside grows inky, like my thoughts, my thoughts.

I am dying for a Twinkie.

Tom is home tonight from Scranton. We curl up on the couch together, under a blanket, whisper I love you, I missed you, confusing tenses I think. Jeffrey comes clunking in on a small broken three-wheeled fire engine.

Dad, Mom said to ask you if I could have a BB gun.

Jeffrey, I say, flabbergasted. I told you you could *not* have a BB gun.

Your mother's right on that score, says Tom, sounding weird—on that score, what the hell is that, he sounds like some oily sportscaster.

Geeze, mutters Jeffrey, maneuvering the firetruck into a three-point turn and back down the hallway. Fuck it damn it all, he says. I am startled.

Watch the mouth, young man, shouts Tom.

During lunch hour today I stop by Mr. Fernandez's school. There are about fifteen kids there and they all seem quiet and good and engrossed in making block forts or cleaning up finger paint. Jeffrey looks up from behind some blocks, yells hi Mom, then resumes work on some precarious architectural project, which is probably also supposed to be a fort. I find a seat nearby and watch. Jeffrey suddenly stands up and looks fidgety, holding his crotch with one hand. Yikes! I gotta go! he shouts and bolts out of the room. While he is in the bathroom, I ask Mr. Fernandez about Jeffrey's language, whether he has noticed anything, any obscenities.

No, says Mr. Fernandez, looking puzzled.

Jeffrey emerges from the john, pulling up his pants.

Amahara chews an office property pen and says, aw, he's probably just reading it on bathroom walls is all.

Fuck it damn it all? He's only four-and-a-half.

Sure, she says, absently cracking plastic between her snaggle teeth. Like: Aint got no toilet paper, fuck it damn it all. Or no nukes, fuck it damn it all. Or no nukes hire the handicapped. Or nuke the handicapped. Or fuck the handicapped, damn it all.

I make a face. Amahara, I say. You're just free-associating.

Best things in life are free, she sighs.

With Amahara, clichés can take on epiphanic dimensions.

Best things in *life are free,* she repeats with emphasis, getting up, casting me a dark glance, and walking out the door, leaves me to wonder what she is driving at.

Tonight by his bed I discover a chewed crayon and a letter Jeffrey has written. It says Dear Jesus and God Hi.

Sunday. This cool cloudless afternoon I feel a pulsing at my neck and head and hips to escape. I drop Jeffrey and Tom off at the cinema for a Disney cartoon fest they both said they wanted to see, and I drive thirty miles or so out into Bucks County toward a gorge and waterfall I read about last summer in an *Inquirer* article entitled, "Nooks for Cooks—Great Spots for the Gourmet Picknicker."

All the way out I listen to the car AM radio, bad lyrics of trailer park love, gin and tonic love, strobe light love, lost and found love, lost and found and lost love, lost and lost and lost love—some people were having no luck at all. The DJ sounds quick and smooth and after-shaved, the rest of the world a mess by comparison.

I have to drive a mile on a narrow string of a dirt road, praying, as my father used to say, like a goddamned mantis that no one will come barreling toward me from the opposite direction. I then leave the car parked at the end of it—along with only one other car—and walk another quarter of a mile in. The trail is black and muddy with spring and as I slop along in old sneakers, I can hear the rush of the water already just a short distance away. Slop City, Batman would say if he were here. Slop, slop.

The trail down from the woods into the gorge is veined with large knobby roots and as I make my way down along them, strategically leaning from tree trunk to tree trunk, it occurs to me that I should be thinking I am too old for this, and yet I am not and instead am marveling, marveling. The smell of the soil is wet and silty and few of the branches of the soft-woods even have buds on them yet. A raccoon, elegantly striped and masked as for a small mammalian ball, has come out of the bushes and approached the creek. I make little noises at it, noises I think might be appropriate raccoon noises: a trilling, clucking

sort of chatter. The raccoon cocks its head to one side, curious.
I try human language—Hey, Mr. Raccoon—and it yammers at
me angrily, scurries away in a furry blur.

In the middle of the creek there are long flat slabs of slate
and I can jump from rock to rock and without much difficulty
land myself in the middle of the largest and sunniest of them.
A few yards down, an old stone bridge spans the gorge, crumbled
but stubborn, its stones chipped and spilled, its mortar cracked;
it is like the weighted arc of a wise mouth, a large, tight-lipped
stitch across the jagged brown banks. I turn from this, turn
toward the shimmer upstream, the bright white of the water, god,
the light of it, as it skis down over the rocks and ragged begin-
nings of mosses, all around the zig-zag of flaking shale, layered
as old pastries. The light, something the article never talked
about, flashing from bud and wave and ripple, everything lined
and measured by it, in this sunken rip, the blinding living ice
of it knocks me out, flat like a lizard on a rock I just lie here
and begin to feel the sun warm my skin even through my clothes,
and then I am taking them off: my jacket, my sneakers, socks,
sweater, pants, underwear. The sun heats the hairs of my goose-
bumps, soaks into my shoulders, the vast incontinent continent
of me; sun closes my eyes, this sun, my sun. The creek roars
around me, waking from winter, strong and renewed. I have
the urge, lying like that, like a fat snake, to squeal or shout.
I stand up and dip my right foot into the creek. No one is around
and I leap from flat rock to flat rock whooping like a cowgirl.
God, you devil you, moments like these I do believe are you, are
gods that hold you and love you happy that's what a god should
do, hold you and love you happy someone is stealing my wallet.

Behind me there is a barebacked man in denim fumbling
with my jacket pocket three rocks away.

I run behind a bush.

Now he is clambering up the slope thinking I haven't
seen him. I can bring myself to say nothing and he gradually

disappears into the trees. I turn away, listen again to the water. I am suddenly getting cold. I go back to my rock and lie down, the earth moving, chafing beneath the blue membrane of the sky like a slow ball-bearing.

I rub my shins and get dressed.

Luckily I still have my keys. On the way back to pick up Jeffrey and Tom from the movie, the radio plays Barbra Streisand movie soundtracks. I take my time. In college there were three books I liked: *Walden, Agamemnon,* and *Waiting for Godot.* These were operations I understood. I hum to the radio. A Smokey the Bear commercial booms on and says that only I can prevent forest fires, I sweat with responsibility, and then the slick, mentholated DJ returns, announcing that now we return to The Way We Were. I drive slow, like an old man after a war.

Sorry I'm late, I yell out the window, parking lot gravel crunching beneath the tires. They are the only two people left at the cinema, and they are standing there like two lone cornstalks by the highway marquee, big and little in navy blue windbreakers. I reach over to unlock the door and they both climb in the front seat, Jeffrey in the middle. Tom slams the door shut.

Sorry I'm late, I say again, and Jeffrey puts one cold hand on my face to try to make me jump and Tom rubs his palms together beneath the glove compartment, saying don't you have the heater on?

I am too warm already, but I flick it to high. It responds with a roar and we are off down the road, a Mayfair dryer on wheels. How was the movie?

Radishes are round, quotes my son. Radishes are red. Specially when you take them and bite off their heads.

That's what Danny the Dragon said, explains my husband.

It wasn't Danny the Dragon, argues Jeffrey. It was the duck that said that.

Tom, I chide, don't you know a duck from a dragon? A light turns yellow and I speed through it.

Tom looks out the window to his right: I'm telling you, it was the dragon.

Jeffrey looks straight ahead. There's no such thing as real dragons, right Mom?

I steal a quick look over his head at Tom, whose nostrils are flaring. We have stopped for a light at Quaker Boulevard. That's right, dear. I think, uh, they were mostly killed off in wars or something.

In the Vietnam war? he asks, so sincere, so interested.

In the War of the Roses, blurts Tom, impatiently, his hands tucked under his arms. Also heavy dragon casualties in the Glorious Revolution.

You'll confuse him, I sing through my teeth, flooring the gas as the light changes.

He's already confused! Tom suddenly shouts, angrily pounding the dashboard as Jeffrey hides his face in my sleeve. I tell you it wasn't the fucking duck!

I've been so touchy, murmurs Tom in bed as we stare at the ceiling together in the dark. I turn my head to look at him. He has been crying. Sharp triangles of hair are plastered to his forehead. Help me, Riva, he gasps, and his face cracks open again, but this time waterlessly. I feel the heaving of his rib cage. He brings his arm up over his face and hides in the angle it forms. I move toward him, on my side, press myself against him, cradle his head, pry loose his arm, and say: Tom, tell me. It's Scranton again, isn't it? He starts to shake his head no but then gives up. He nods yes and somehow it helps lessen the heaving. His eyes look at me, frantic, desperate. I place my hand gently to his cheek, but I do not kiss him.

I am sure the lady at the health food store is dying. Her eyes are puffy and her lips are dried, stuck together. If she opened her mouth, it would sound like Velcro pulling apart. The door clacks and tinkles behind me.

Hi, I say cheerily. Well, you know, guess what, Scranton's back in the picture again that tenacious dame. What can you do? No water can be thicker than water, you know what I mean?

I have no idea what I'm saying. I just want to save her life.

Tom's okay, I continue. I mean, we all have our bad habits. Me, for instance, I eat graham crackers like crazy.

Her mouth lets in air, a grinning fish. Sorry to hear that, she says.

But I don't know whether she means Scranton or the graham crackers, and so I just say yeah, well, I'm sure I need some sort of vitamin, and look woefully toward the shelf.

Amahara, can you come here please and take care of Mrs. Baker's account?

That old bag?

I grimace. Mrs. Baker is standing not six feet away. What I mean, Amahara recovers impressively, picking up a marked-down patent leather purse and smiling at Mrs. Baker, is that you really do need a new bag.

Perhaps I should do something else. Teach or something, I am saying to my mother who has relapsed into senility again but who is demanding that I confide professional and domestic secrets. She will insist she doesn't remember a thing, that I should tell her my troubles again. She already has forgotten her announced intention to leave St. Veronica's.

Has this Tom got a new mistress? she asks sternly, as if that would explain my discontent with Leigenbaum's.

No, no. That's not it, I say quickly and turn the subject to the gum she is chewing, which smells like suntan lotion.

Honey-coconut, she says. No problem with my dentures either.

There is a long silence. I look at my hands.

Good stuff, reiterates my mother. Honey-coconut. Made by Beech-Nut.

Why do you haunt me? You, like a tattoo on my tongue, like the bay leaf at the bottom of every pan. You who sprawled out beside me and sang my horoscope to a Schubert symphony, something about travel and money again, and we lay there, both of our breaths bad, both of our underwear dangling elastic, and then you turned toward me with a gaze like two matches, putting the horoscope aside, you traced my buried ribs with an index finger, lingered at my collarbone, admiring it as one might a flying buttress, murmuring: Nice clavicle. And me, too new at it and scared, not knowing what to say, whispering: You should see my ten-speed.

Jeffrey get in here, I yell out the back door. It's getting dark and dinner's ready. He is playing Murder the Leaf in the backyard with his friend Angela Dillersham. They carry large sticks.

Jeffrey do you hear me?

Yeah, he says and mumbles see ya to Angela, then shambles toward the back porch. Fuck it, damn it all, I hear him say, dragging himself up the stairs and I slap him as he comes in the door and send him crying to his room without his spaghetti or his fruit cocktail or his stick.

Where's Jeffrey? asks Tom.

He's being punished, I say, twirling spaghetti into a spoon.

But you sent him to bed without dinner two nights ago, says Tom, petulantly poking a wrinkled grape. Fuck it, damn it all, Riva, he's going to starve if you keep this up.

Go to your room, Tom, I say.

But he doesn't. He stays. He looks at me, blinking and amazed.

We are in Tom's room. My curtains and my clothes are here, but more and more it has taken on a disgruntled greenish-ness that is Tom's, a foggy haze like a fish tank that needs to be cleaned. We have to talk about this, he says.

What is *this*? I ask.

Scranton. Julia. You know. It's at the root of it all.

It all? I ask, a tyrant for precision.

Yes, well, this giant ravine between us, he explains.

Ah yes. Ravine. I think of my stolen wallet. There were pictures. And an eye donor's card. And then I think of the sun, the son.

I'm sure it's hard for you to believe, he continues. After all I said and promised last year and now all this . . . again . . .

All *this*? I ask, getting good at it.

Julia.

Oh, right. Scranton. I have always hated her name.

You must feel you're caught up in some vicious cycle. His voice sounds kind, sympathetic. At least I know I do, he is saying.

Cycle? I feel sarcasm flying up into my throat, shrill and inarticulate as a blue jay. Vicious cycle? I shout again. Hey. Listen. You should see my ten-speed.

I grow incomprehensible.

Easter. We try not to make too much of it. Jeffrey finds all the beans, saves me the purple ones. The air's warming, it's hard to sleep, and caterpillars sound like wind munching, denuding the spring trees. The days smell like a hamster cage, leaf bits lit-tering the walks.

I long for you, I short for you, I wear shorts for you.

Jeffrey eats all his dinner tonight. He has been sweet all day, brought me a potato print of what he calls the *limpbirdie* bell. Before bed I read him a story about a Mexican boy and a pinata, and Jeffrey says: Am I gonna do that, too, Mom? Smash my horse pinata? And I say that his horse pinata is different, it's a gift from Mr. Fernandez, and it's supposed to just hang there and not be broken. He yawns and stumbles off to plunk and deedle-dee, his sound words—where has he gotten this other stuff from?

Is God a giant like Hercules? asks Jeffrey just before drifting off. And I sit at the bed's edge and say God's a giant like the sun or like the sky, a huge blanket that all the planets are swimming in.

Could Hercules kill a gorilla? asks Jeffrey.

I slather heavy peach makeup over the rash by my mouth and go to see Mr. Fernandez at the lunch hour again. He insists Jeffrey is fine, although I'm still worried about his language. I sit next to Mr. Fernandez at a low, made-for-kids table, watching Jeffrey and the others play. He notices I am glum and places his hand on mine, says nothing.

Mr. Fernandez, I ask him finally. Are you happy?

He looks straight ahead for a minute.

Riva, he says, at last. You're not asking the right questions.

What's a right question?

Ah, he says mysteriously.

Ah? I ask. It sounds like tonsilitis. He nods, grins through his beard.

A little girl with short hair pale as the inside of a lemon rind runs up and places her cheek against Mr. Fernandez's knee. She has wet brown cookie remnants at the corner of her mouth. Can I have some juice now, please? she asks, running her fingers up and down the corduroy grooves of his thigh. She stops and looks up at me quizzically. A tiny cookie bit falls from her mouth. What kind of juice do you like? I ask her, solicitous, false-friendly, ridiculous.

She looks at me, knits her brows, takes Mr. Fernandez's

hand, and turns away, pulling him toward the refrigerator at the far end of the room. He looks at me and shrugs and I shrug back. Not asking the right questions.

Things seem tense at work. People are wooden, scarcely polite, their eyes like fruit pits.

In bed with Tom. He holds me. I am sorry, he says. I love you. I love Jeffrey, I love that kid.
So do I, I say carefully.
There's a long moment before he says: What should we do? Do you want a divorce?
You are my husband, I say with difficulty, like a stroke victim, my tongue plugged in my throat like a scarf or a handbag.

I'm thinking of writing an herb book, says the woman in the health food store. Her hair lies in unwashed strings on the shoulders of her pink-gray sweater and against the pink-gray slope of her face.
It's good to have a project, I say, trying to sound cheerful, encouraging. Something to live with, something to always return to.
Something you love, she says, and holds up a green sprig of something, looks at me, smiles weakly.

Today I did a thousand dollars.
Things. Sometimes you just have to do them.

What do you want to be when you grow up, Jeffrey? I ask, chopping squash, squashing chops.
A car driver.
A car driver?
Yeah, you drive cars, he says and starts to zoom around the kitchen, three-point turning into cupboards.

Jeffrey, come and stir this brownie mix for me.

Okay, he says obediently, and we sit next to each other on stools at the counter. He is fidgety, restless. I push his hair back out of his face with my one clean hand. I can cradle his whole head with it, it seems.

What do *you* want me to be when I grow up? he asks, stirring, licking a fingertip.

I want you to be good.

I'm good at potato prints, he says, my earnest little potato prince.

No, I don't mean good *at* something, I mean just plain good. Being just plain good.

I'm good, he says.

You're good, I smile, mussing up his hair and smoothing it down again.

He reaches up, plays with my earring. I like it when you get dressed up, Mommy, he says.

I step out of the bathroom with nothing on.

Well, Tom, Sergeant, babydollbaby. Do I get into a prone position? A provolone position? I lumber into bed like a mammoth cheese.

Tom reaches under the covers and clasps my hand. Riva, I'm worried about you. Everything's a joke. You're always flip-flopping words, only listening to the edge of things. It's like you're always, constantly, on the edge.

Life is a pun, I say. It's something that sounds like one thing but also sounds like even means like something else.

Riva, what you just said. It's empty. It doesn't mean anything. He says this with a sort of tender reluctance, as if it were the last thing in the world he wanted to do.

It doesn't? I ask, suddenly embarrassed, confused, thinking that there is so much sanity in the insurance business. I slide down into the bed, press my face into his ribs, his strong ribs, the health food lady, I think, should have these ribs against her

Velcro lips for a night, just a night, and then it occurs to me that maybe she already has.

I have brought my mother roses and a Tolkien trilogy. She smiles weakly, then lays them aside. Now, what was his name again? she asks, pouring ice water into a glass.

In the Leigenbaum's employees' ladies' room, someone has written: I'm a virgin what is wrong with me? Beneath that, other people have written a string of feminist graffiti to reassure her, and underneath that, someone else has written in huge red letters: I don't care if I'm a fish, I still want a bicycle.

By the scarves, a woman asks me skeptically about designer names. I go into my rap about differences in French and Italian mills and also about supporting living working artists.

Do you think it really matters if you get laid in a Pucci scarf rather than one by somebody else? she asks.

I stare at her nose, tough as a root. You get laid in scarves? I finally say.

There are problems with these receipts, says the district manager, who is in for the day, on an official visit. Amahara is sitting next to him, not looking at me, her face blank as a window shade. I have just been called into the office.

I'm not sure what you mean, I say.

I think you are, he says. We could get into accusations here of gross negligence or outright criminal behavior. But the outcome would be the same. I don't know what sort of stress you've been under, but, Riva, you are fired. Without severance pay. You can pack your stuff and leave this afternoon.

Excuse me? I ask, not at all the right question, for he gets up and leaves without answering, Amahara close behind.

A smoky, hot pretzel smell in the city of blubbery love. A woman with jam on her plastic arm is attracting bees in Rittenhouse Square. Steam jostles the manhole covers, traffic resetting them, flat, flush, a regular metallic thud. The dusty burn of subway wafts up from concrete descents, and a peddler with a hint of mange at the hairline shouts fourteen carat, twenty at Bonwit's we'll give it to you for ten. Music grows loud and near, then fades and is gone, a casual invasion, hasty imprint and flight like the path of a bullet. I wander the streets frowsy and bloated, a W. C. Fields in drag, my mascara smeared like coal around my eyes, in store windows it is hard to recognize myself. I walk into places and flip through the racks, then leave, not really seeing too much, people spinning through doors, buzzing by me. They have drunk too much coffee. Caterpillars crawl the edge of the sidewalks like chromosomes. Looking for food, I roam slowly.

At Beefsteak Charley's I stop to blindly read the menu and the poster for the circus and suddenly notice Tom inside eating. He is with a thin, dark-haired woman and Jeffrey, whom he wasn't supposed to pick up from Mr. Fernandez's until six. The circus clown grins.

I pull the door open, walk in. It is fairly empty. In the center is a giant salad bar island with sneeze guards. They must have three kinds of macaroni salad here.

Tom looks up and is a bit taken aback at seeing me. Riva, he says unimaginatively. I thought you were working late tonight.

Hi Mom, chirps Jeffrey, his mouth full of corn relish and pickled beets. Look what Julia gave me. He points to the blue University of Kentucky T-shirt he is wearing.

Neat, I say.

I went to graduate school there, smiles the brunette.

Oh, introductions, says Tom, a bit frantic. Riva, this is Julia. Julia is a poet, he says hopefully. She teaches in Scranton.

Yes, I've heard, I say, my eye in third gear, hives blooming, lumps forming under my skin, near my mouth, ready to be lanced. How do you do? It sounds like the right question. I continue: I've never met a skinny poet before.

Tom looks at me oddly, vaguely yellow. Julia smiles sweet as cake.

Tom, can I talk to you for a moment? I ask, still standing, and he says sure and we walk together back toward the entrance by the unmanned cash register and a phone and extra menus and matches with "What's Your Beef?" printed on them, and I place my pocketbook in the after-dinner mints, slowly reach for a steak knife from an empty table and when he says what are you doing, what is it, I look at his murky hairline receding like a tide and I say you are my goddamned husband and jam the knife hard into his ribs.

It doesn't seem to go very far, like something thrust into a radiator, but I let go and it sticks there for a long moment, then falls toward the carpet like a small, dumb, wingless bat. Tom's face is a horrible orgasm with eyes. He slumps toward the phone, lifts the receiver, slowly begins dialing 911, blood splotching onto his white shirt like cardinals in the snow, or sunburned nuns, I have lost my mind there is now I realize some commotion, some howling about the place, waiters in bow ties have come out from the kitchen and Julia flushed and murmuring like a very true poet holy fuck it damn it all comes stumbling over and the little University of Kentucky is frozen in his chair clutching a forkful of corn relish, his face a terrified marshmallow, oh my god, my god, I whisper into my hands.

You'll never see Jeffrey again, murmurs Tom, you can count on that, the pain on Tom's face, in his chest something enormous and sad, and then he is giving information to the operator and soon there are sirens.

I have my own room. Someone has sent me flowers. Is it you, Phil, who could it be, thinking of me?

Mr. Fernandez drops by to see me at St. Veronica's during visiting hours.

Do you realize, he says, that there's a nuclear bomb hanging over each and every one of us like a monster pinata?

I begin to understand his metaphors.

And you go off and do this, he says. Who the hell do you think you are?

I think to myself that this must be the right sort of question, the sort one is supposed to ask.

Pride cometh before the fall, I say, lost, foundering. Sometimes in May.

He leans over and kisses me. Riva, he says. I saw your husband today. He's fine but says he and Jeffrey will not come to see you.

I look out the windows, at gray, gray buildings, and say shit, and then start crying. I am crying, I can't help it.

I brought you a treat, Mr. Fernandez says, holding me with one arm and handing me a cheese danish wrapped in cellophane.

I blow my nose, unwrap the danish, break off part and push it in my mouth. I'm bonkers, aren't I? I ask with my mouth full.

You're unhappy, says Mr. Fernandez. It can be the same thing. You are unhappy because you believe in such a thing as happy.

I stop eating. I feel sick. This danish is too sweetish to finish, I say, a little Scandinavian humor, and fillip the crumbs off the bedsheets.

I'm going to leave you now. I just stopped by for a minute.

I look at his magic Jesus beard and panic. Please don't go.

I'll stop by tomorrow, he says gently.

Thank you, I say, never more grateful for anything in my whole life.

Orderlies roll the days by me like carts.

Mr. Fernandez visits, but only him. My husband and son are off someplace, walking and trying not to cry.

———————

Aging flowers, daisies when they die look like hopeful hags, their sunny, hatless faces, their shriveled, limp hair. Tulips wither into birdcages, six black stamens inside, each dried to a dim chirp.

The gray buildings fill my windows, my gibbering with salt: Who were you ever? An apoplexy to fill my days, to fill my insomnia with your insomnia, my bard of lard, my long ago husband, sometimes I think I made you up, but sometimes I think you live close, in this city, in my house, buried in the cellar or in paperwork and business trips, rising up at night like a past repast I can wish to death: Please die.

My mother is two floors above me. It would be humorous, but it's not humorous. We are allowed finally to meet in our bathrobes in the coffee shop downstairs.

Well, I say, quoting Humphrey Bogart in a line to Ingrid Bergman at a table at Rick's: I guess neither one of our stories is very funny.

Riva, she says. Your father was a madman. He used to punch cars and threaten to swallow things. Maybe you inherited his genes.

I like to swallow things, I say.

Today is Friday. The nuns are friendlier, my eye flickless, my skin, body, brighter, thinner. I take an afternoon nap and dream bittersweetly that all the friends I've ever had march in here to see how I am.

When I wake up, Sister Henrietta knocks at my door and says a gentleman is here to see you, Riva.

I am disoriented from my dream, quickly straighten my hair, and say, as in the movies, Sister, you can send him in now. I turn to look out the window: the gray buildings of my life, the gray buildings.

And it is Jeffrey who appears in the doorway. He hangs there small and alone. Mom? he squeaks, then steps closer to the bed. He is wearing an oversized U. of Penn T-shirt, twisting and wringing at the bottom of it with one hand. Hi, Mom, he says.

My hips ache. My eyes burn happy sad happy. Nice shirt there, Batman, I say.

He tugs at it. Dad says this is where you went to college, he says, too far away for me to touch his arm.

How have you been doing, Jeffrey? I ask.

I broke my pinata, he says. I just broke it open, he shrugs, gulps, a small wrenching glug, looks at the ceiling. And there was nothing in it, he adds. But there's a circus coming pretty soon. There's gonna be a circus.

He stands there, away from me, afraid, holding his fingers. I am strange to him. Perhaps he thinks I have turned into Gramma.

Mom, are you my friend? he asks, barely audible, his face pale and homeless.

I nod yes.

Are you my mother?

I nod again, smiling, and he thinks about this, then approaches me, reaches and climbs up into my lap, curls into my breasts, clutching my gown, bursts into tears, his face crumpling against me. I want to go to the circus and see the horse people, he cries, wet and red, and I hold him close, warm, in my arms, in this room, and tell him we will go.

A NOTE ON THE TYPE

The text of this book was set on the Linotype in a type face
known as Garamond. The design is based on letter forms
originally created by Claude Garamond (ca. 1480–1561).
Garamond was a pupil of Geoffroy Tory and may have pat-
terned his letter form on Venetian models. To this day, the
type face that bears his name is one of the most attractive
used in book composition, and the intervening years have
caused it to lose little of its freshness or beauty.

Composed by Maryland Linotype Composition Company,
Baltimore, Maryland
Printed and bound by Fairfield Graphics,
Fairfield, Pennsylvania

Designed by Tasha Hall